When he saw her he got to his feet, whispering so as not to disturb Amy. 'Sorry. The door was open…'

'That's okay. When I heard about the accident I held her a little tighter.'

'We have to protect her.'

'We will.'

He'd settled for want, instead of need, and gone upstairs to check on Amy. But now that Chloe was here… Jon reminded himself that she had her own issues about being touched, and that the intensity with which he wanted to touch her would probably be unwelcome.

But she touched him. He drew away and she touched him again, taking hold of the front of his shirt and pulling him towards her. And then she was in his arms. Chloe reached out, curling her fingers around his neck.

One breath. One look.

There was no longer any him or her—just one frozen moment in time which they both c_____ _____ Chl__ _____ ___'and e_____ _____ uestion a___

Dear Reader,

There are times when I dream of perfection. But in reality I know that it *is* just a dream. Because, to me, a world without any flaws would hold no challenge—nothing to strive for. And perhaps it's the way we deal with situations which are less than perfect that is the truest measure of our spirit and humanity.

So a hero who wants perfection isn't someone I'd normally see eye to eye with. Perhaps that's why I gave Dr Jon Lambert a particularly hard time in this book, throwing him together with a heroine who resists taking the help he offers and facing them both with a situation that tests Jon to the limit. But, like any true hero, Jon has it in him to rise to the challenge—even if it does mean that he's forced to re-examine his perspective on life.

When Chloe Delancourt's niece, baby Amy, is in danger of being abandoned by her mother, Chloe must fight to reunite her family and secure Amy's future. Jon isn't her first choice of ally, but she has no choice but to admit she needs his help. And in working together to save baby Amy both Jon and Chloe discover that perfection isn't something either of them needs in order to find true happiness and fulfilment.

Thank you for reading Jon and Chloe's story. I'm always thrilled to hear from readers, and you can contact me via my website at annieclaydon.com

Annie x

SAVING BABY AMY

BY
ANNIE CLAYDON

All rights reserved including the right of reproduction in whole or in part in any form. This edition is published by arrangement with Harlequin Books S.A.

This is a work of fiction. Names, characters, places, locations and incidents are purely fictional and bear no relationship to any real life individuals, living or dead, or to any actual places, business establishments, locations, events or incidents. Any resemblance is entirely coincidental.

This book is sold subject to the condition that it shall not, by way of trade or otherwise, be lent, resold, hired out or otherwise circulated without the prior consent of the publisher in any form of binding or cover other than that in which it is published and without a similar condition including this condition being imposed on the subsequent purchaser.

® and TM are trademarks owned and used by the trademark owner and/or its licensee. Trademarks marked with ® are registered with the United Kingdom Patent Office and/or the Office for Harmonisation in the Internal Market and in other countries.

Published in Great Britain 2017
By Mills & Boon, an imprint of HarperCollins*Publishers*
1 London Bridge Street, London, SE1 9GF

© 2017 Annie Claydon

ISBN: 978-0-263-92657-6

Our policy is to use papers that are natural, renewable and recyclable products and made from wood grown in sustainable forests. The logging and manufacturing processes conform to the legal environmental regulations of the country of origin.

Printed and bound in Spain
by CPI, Barcelona

Cursed with a poor sense of direction and a propensity to read, **Annie Claydon** spent much of her childhood lost in books. A degree in English Literature followed by a career in computing didn't lead directly to her perfect job—writing romance for Mills & Boon—but she has no regrets in taking the scenic route. She lives in London: a city where getting lost can be a joy.

Books by Annie Claydon

Mills & Boon Medical Romance

Stranded in His Arms

Rescued by Dr Rafe
Saved by the Single Dad

The Doctor She'd Never Forget
Discovering Dr Riley
The Doctor's Diamond Proposal
English Rose for the Sicilian Doc

Visit the Author Profile page
at millsandboon.co.uk for more titles.

To Rosie, with love.

CHAPTER ONE

HOSPITAL GOSSIP WAS a bit like the wind: unpredictable and prone to sudden gusts in one direction or another. Information could easily end up at the furthest corner of the hospital before it came to the notice of the people involved. So it was no particular surprise to Chloe Delancourt that she'd walked all the way over to the canteen before hearing a piece of news that quite obviously pertained to her.

'So what's all this about your boyfriend and a baby?' One of the other junior doctors joined her at the end of the queue.

'*My* boyfriend?' Jake was long gone, and if he did have a baby it was nothing to do with her.

Petra grinned. 'All right, so he's not your boyfriend. Since he's good looking, single and living with you, that might be classed as an omission on your part.'

'You mean Jon?' Chloe had only seen Dr Jonathan Lambert for a total of about ten minutes since he'd moved in two weeks ago.

'How many good-looking men are you living with currently?'

'Just the one…' The ten minutes had been more than enough to notice that he *was* good looking. And that he had a delicious smile. But apart from that all she really knew about him was that he was a good friend of her brother's and he kept the bathroom tidy. He'd started his new job at the hospital six weeks earlier than anticipated and had needed a place to stay because the renovations on his own house weren't finished yet.

'Glad to hear it. If there was more than one of them, I'd be looking for an invitation to come over for dinner at the weekend.'

Chloe shrugged. 'Come over anyway, I'm not doing anything tomorrow. It'll be just the two of us, though, he's not exactly made his presence felt.'

'If he's working nights then I suppose you wouldn't see much of him during the week…' Petra was obviously turning the idea over in her head.

'Or the weekend. He spends every waking hour over at his place. I've hardly seen him.' Maybe Jon *was* avoiding her. Or maybe he just took the promise that she'd hardly know he was there very seriously. Whatever. It suited Chloe not to get too involved with a face as handsome as his.

'Well, he's here now. With a baby.'

'What kind of baby?'

Petra rolled her eyes. 'Two arms, two legs…the usual. A little girl, he was calling her Amy…'

'What?' Chloe almost dropped her tray and instead thrust it into Petra's hands. 'Where is he?'

'He was in A and E about five minutes ago. Someone said he'd asked for directions up to Orthopaedics—.' Petra broke off as Chloe turned, running for the doors of the canteen.

Chloe had sprinted across the courtyard and up three flights of stairs, back to her own department. Jon had been up to Orthopaedics and left a message that he was going back downstairs to A and E. By the time she got down to the Paediatric A and E department she could hardly breathe so it was just as well that the receptionist knew what she wanted without Chloe having to say so.

'That was quick, I've only just paged you. They've just gone through. Consulting Room Three.'

The pager in Chloe's pocket buzzed suddenly and she jumped, switching it off. Taking a deep breath, in an effort to slow her racing heart, she thanked the receptionist and walked slowly towards the consulting rooms.

If Amy was here, then where was Hannah? And if Hannah had left her child with Jon that posed a whole slew of other questions that Chloe really didn't want to think about until she was sure of the situation. She knocked and turned the handle of the consulting-room door before whoever was inside had a chance to answer.

Jon was lifting Amy out of her car seat. He'd obviously dressed quickly, because his shirt was buttoned up wrong, leaving one red checked tail slightly longer than the other at the front. Amy fretted a little, and then seemed to decide that the strong cradle of Jon's arms was a safe place.

'What...?'

She hadn't noticed how blue his eyes were before, or how tender. Or that his light brown hair, falling across his brow, gave him a slightly boyish look. Or that his hands seemed so large and capable next to Amy's tiny fingers.

'Sit down.' Amy stirred slightly at Jon's words, and then snuggled back against his chest. For a moment it seemed the best place in the world to be. Held in his arms without a care in the world.

But if Amy didn't seem concerned about the where-abouts of her mother, Chloe was. 'Where's my sister?'

'Hannah's at your place.' The tenderness in his eyes seemed reserved just for Amy, and he gave Chloe a more dispassionate look. 'Sit…'

Clearly something was up, and he wasn't going to tell her until she was sitting down. She bit back the temptation to tell him that she was a doctor too, and that she'd been working at this hospital a good deal longer than he had. Even if she did feel far more like a slightly panicky aunt than a doctor at the moment.

The dark blue windcheater on the chair next to him had been hanging in her hallway for the past two weeks, and was probably the most familiar thing about him. Chloe moved it, draping it over the backrest. When she sat down, an elusive hint of his scent halted the clamour of her senses for a moment, as if they'd paused to appreciate it. This wasn't the time, or the place…

His eyes and the slight curve of his lips invited calm. No… Actually, they invited surrender, and that wasn't something that Chloe was prepared to give. 'Tell me what's happened.'

'Hannah was worried about Amy and she took her to her own doctor this morning. He told her that Amy just had a virus, but Hannah thought it was something more so she brought her to you.'

'And…?' Chloe reached across to feel Amy's forehead. She was a little feverish, and her cheeks were flushed.

'I agreed with Hannah. So I brought Amy here, where she could be examined and treated properly.'

'But where's Hannah?' Chloe couldn't keep the frustration from her voice.

'She's at your place. She was…a little distressed.'

'A little distressed?' Chloe frowned at him. Jon didn't need to play the situation down for her benefit.

'She was crying her eyes out, and she insisted on staying behind while I brought Amy here.' Chloe's eyebrows shot up and he flashed her a cool smile. 'It's okay. I got to know Hannah quite well when she was staying with James. She wasn't entrusting Amy to a stranger.'

So, however distressed Hannah was, she was still thinking straight. That was something. James had mentioned that a friend of his had helped out a lot with Hannah, spending time with her and letting her talk, but Chloe hadn't realised it was Jon.

But if Hannah had found someone to talk to in Jon, then Chloe couldn't see how. He seemed somehow distant, as if Amy was the only person in the room he could trust with an unreserved smile.

'Then you'll know that Hannah's...vulnerable.' Chloe twisted her lips. Vulnerable wasn't quite the right word. Hannah could be surprisingly strong and very determined. But she was young. Troubled sometimes.

'I know that she's almost ten years younger than you, and that she was only nine when you lost both your parents. That you and James have done your best to look after her, but it hasn't always been easy.'

'No, it hasn't.' Chloe hadn't made it any easier. Hannah had always wanted to live with her, and Chloe had worked hard, saving every penny she could and adding to her third of the money from the sale of their parents' house so that she could afford a home for the two of them. She'd bought the house, and then two months after they'd moved in Chloe had fallen ill. Hannah had gone to live with James instead, but had never really settled.

'Look, Hannah's okay for the moment.'

Okay for the moment. Most people had learned to

settle for that where Hannah was concerned, but Chloe wanted more for her sister.

'You do know that Hannah's still only eighteen? And that Amy's father isn't on the scene?' Hannah had run away two weeks before her sixteenth birthday. Chloe had been too ill to do anything but worry, while James had moved heaven and earth to find their sister. When he had, she'd been living with a boy of nineteen, who had been more than eager to give her up when James had wondered aloud whether Hannah's queasy spells might be morning sickness.

'Yes, I know. She's all right.' It seemed that Chloe was going to have to take his word for it, because Jon's face showed no evidence that he really understood the gravity of the situation. His whole attention was focussed on Amy.

'I'd just feel a bit better if she were here and I could see for myself.' Her words sounded rather more accusing than Chloe had meant them to.

'I felt that Amy needed to be looked at sooner rather than later, and that was my first priority. Hannah calmed down when she saw I was taking her concerns seriously and promised to stay put while I was gone.'

'Yes… I'm sorry. Thanks.' None of this was Jon's fault. Hannah had put him in a difficult position and he'd taken the only decision he could. Chloe stretched her arms out towards Amy. 'I'll take her now.'

He didn't move. 'Why don't you let me examine her? I can do it now—my shift won't be starting for another three hours.'

'And you're better qualified than me?' There was something he wasn't saying, and Chloe guessed it might be that. It was true, after all. Jon's speciality was paediatric emergencies, and even though he'd only been here a couple of weeks he was already gaining something of a reputation as an excellent doctor.

'Yes, I am. And I'm not Amy's aunt.' He said the words dispassionately. 'I dare say you're a lot better at dealing with Hannah than I am. Why don't you give her a call, while I fetch my stethoscope from my locker?'

Maybe he was just giving her something to do to keep her quiet, because it seemed that he had already come to some kind of agreement with Hannah. But he was right. Chloe nodded and Jon delivered Amy into her arms.

'She's two years old. All of her immunisations are up to date and she's on no medication.' If she was going to take up the role of concerned aunt then she may as well give Jon all the relevant information. And ask the relevant questions. 'What do you think?'

'I don't know anything for sure yet.' He got to his feet and walked out of the room, without looking back.

Jon had woken to the sound of the front door banging closed, and had got out of bed, groggily thinking that he must have overslept if Chloe was home already. And then he'd heard Amy crying and had gone downstairs to find that it was Hannah.

He shouldn't really have been there at all. But the hospital had asked him to fill in for someone who was sick, six weeks before he was due to start his new job there, and he'd had to find a place to stay in the area. Chloe's place wasn't ideal as it reminded him too much of the family that he'd never again be a part of. But the renovations on the new house he'd bought had been the perfect excuse to stay out of her way and only return to her place to get some sleep while she was at work.

Although he'd seen little of Chloe herself, the slightly

shabby, eclectic warmth of her home surrounded him.
He slept between her sheets, saw her bottles in the bathroom when he went to take a shower and her food in
the fridge when he went downstairs to make coffee.
And if love had been something he ever wanted to do
again, he would already have been a little in love with
Chloe's scent.

But that wasn't an option. He walked back into the
consulting room, armed to the teeth with all the rea-
sons why he shouldn't get involved with Chloe. She was
cuddling Amy in her lap, her phone tucked against her
shoulder, her brow creased in concentration.

'Yes, don't worry, we'll make absolutely sure she's
all right. What about you?'

A pause, and then her lips twitched into a smile. It
seemed that whatever was being said at the other end
of the line was a reassurance.

'Okay. You'll stay there until I get back. Promise?
Yeah, love you too.' Chloe caught her phone as it slid
from her ear and ended the call.

'Hannah?'

'Yes. She sounds all right, but she won't come to
the hospital. She says…' Chloe shook her head. 'She's
so terrified that she's not doing well enough, and that
people will think she's a bad mother.'

Jon nodded. It wasn't the first time he'd heard that
particular sentiment, and it was ironic that it was often
the most loving and capable mothers who voiced it.
But, then, family relationships weren't exactly his forte.

'First things first. I'll take a look at Amy.' That he
could do, and he knew he could do it well.

He was aware that Chloe's gaze was on him, an in-
trusion that felt so warm and welcome that all he could
do was try to shut it out. Amy was fretting a little, obvi-

ously out of sorts, and he concentrated on soothing her, trying to make the examination into a game.

'I think she may have a urinary tract infection.' Finally he turned and faced Chloe.

'Why?'

A fair enough question. She was a doctor too, and he couldn't completely relegate her to the role of faceless care-giver. 'She has a fever, but there's no sign of a cold. Her blood pressure is slightly high, which is a concern, and...' He shrugged. 'I changed her nappy pants before I brought her here.'

'And?'

This was the part where instinct corroborated medical fact. 'There's a particular smell that can point to a UTI in young children. Not always, but it's an indicator.'

She nodded and Jon thought he saw her lips purse slightly. Maybe it was just his imagination. 'Is that an old wives' tale?'

'It was something that a very experienced health visitor told me when I was starting out. It's been statistically confirmed since.'

'Which means you need a mid-stream urine sample?'

'Yes. I think I can get that the natural way, without having to catheterise her.'

He passed this test every day. Concerned parents, who needed to know whether they could really trust him or not. It was only right that care-givers should question him and weigh everything he did up for themselves, but it was different with Chloe. He wanted very badly to make her smile.

Suddenly she did, and the effect left him momentarily transfixed, taking in all the tiny details that he'd forced himself not to notice before. The way her light auburn hair, scraped back away from her face, escaped in curls around her brow. The tiny freckles across her nose, and her pale skin. Long legs encased in a neat, business-like skirt. She was the kind of woman that a man could spend a lot of time watching.

She reddened slightly—enchantingly—and Jon looked away quickly. It was nothing. He was human, and it was just an echo from a long-gone past, when wanting to watch every move a woman made had been something that might lead somewhere.

'Did your very experienced health visitor give you any clues about how to get a two-year-old to pee on demand?'

'As it happens, no. But I've picked up a few pointers from their mothers. And I gave her a drink as soon as I got here.'

He bent over Amy, smiling at her, and she rewarded him with a smile in return. That's what he liked so much about children, they were usually a lot less complicated than adults. 'Right, young lady. Let's give this a go.'

CHAPTER TWO

HE WAS SO good with Amy. Confident, gentle and play-ful. The kind of doctor that every parent wanted to see when their child was sick. Chloe knew that a mid-stream urine sample, one that wasn't contaminated by any bacteria from the skin, wasn't an easy proposition, and she waited to see what Jon was going to come up with.

He didn't disappoint. Taking Amy's nappy pants off and cleaning her carefully, he made a game out of sit-ting her on a potty and splashing her hands and feet in a bowl of warm water. Even though she was fretful and drowsy, he somehow managed to make her drink a little more and make her laugh at the faces he pulled. When she did finally give in, he seized the opportunity and deftly caught a mid-stream sample in the small con-tainer he had ready.

'Well done, sweetheart.' He hugged Amy and she grabbed at the sample bottle, almost spilling its precious contents. Chloe took it from him, snapping the lid on firmly, and Jon set about dressing Amy.

'The urinalysis test kits are over there.' He nod-ded towards a cupboard in the corner of the consult-ing room.

It seemed that, finally, she was going to be allowed

to do something, instead of sitting and watching Jon
work. Even if sitting and watching him did have its
good points. Chloe carefully divided the small sample
into two, one for the lab, if needed, and the other for
the test strip from the urinalysis kit.

'You were right.' She showed the coloured test strip
to Jon and his brow darkened. There was a clear indi-
cation of the presence of white blood cells and bacteria.

'I think it's best if we take her into the children's
ward, for tonight at least. The infection's clearly putting her under some stress.'

And Amy's home situation wasn't ideal at the moment. At least he had the delicacy not to mention that.
Or maybe he was just ignoring it, since that was Chloe's
problem, not his.

'Yes, I agree. Thanks, Jon.'

'Are you finished for the day?'

Chloe nodded. 'Yes, I've seen all the patients on
my list. I had some paperwork to catch up on but that
can wait.'

'Then what do you say to my staying here with Amy
and sorting out a bed for her? I think it's time you went
home and had a conversation with Hannah.'

He was absolutely right and wishing that Jon would
come with her, in the hope that he might be able to con-
quer Hannah's fears as effortlessly as he'd conquered
Amy's, was just selfish. Amy needed someone with her
here, and Hannah needed some support too. This was
the obvious solution.

'Are you sure? I don't know how long I'll be.'

'I'm fine here until my shift starts. You'll be back
by then?'

'Yes, I'll make sure if it. With or without Hannah.' A
thought occurred to her. 'Have you eaten?' He shook his

head, as if that didn't really matter. 'I'll get you something. I've got some rosehip teabags if you'd like tea?'

From the look on his face, rosehip teabags didn't quite hit the spot. 'Thanks, but…actually anything with caffeine and a few calories would be great. And a drink for Amy. My wallet's in my jacket pocket.'

He picked Amy up, soothing her gently. Chloe ignored his jacket and made for the door. The least she could do for him was to stand him breakfast, even if it was just a sandwich from the canteen.

Chloe had left a large cup of coffee and a sandwich from the canteen perched on the window sill, well out of Amy's reach. Then she'd hugged Amy, gifted Jon with a smile that had been as delicious as it had been hurried, and had left.

'Just you and me, then, eh?' He rocked Amy in his arms. She was becoming increasingly fretful, and the sooner he started the antibiotic drip the better. He'd sent one of the nurses to get what he needed, and he was alone for a moment.

'Don't you worry, now, sweetheart. Everything's going to be okay, and we'll make you better.' Making Amy better was reasonably straightforward. Making everything okay was a lot more fraught with uncertainty. Hannah hadn't just been distressed when she'd arrived at Chloe's house, there had been a wild look in her eyes that had told Jon she was very close to breaking point. He'd been loath to leave her alone, but Hannah hadn't given him much choice in the matter.

'Mum-eee…' Amy's little face started to scrunch up and tears escaped her eyes. Jon held her close, soothing her.

'All right. Mummy's coming.' Not straight away but soon, he hoped. 'You want to know a secret, Amy?'

'I love secrets...' Jon jumped as someone spoke. He hadn't heard the calm-faced nurse re-enter the room, and when he turned she was standing behind him.

'This one is that I'm gasping for that cup of coffee over there.' Jon gave her a smile and a shrug when her lip curled slightly in disbelief.

'I'll take her. Go and drink your coffee.'

'Thanks.'

He'd leave the real secret until later. It was one thing to tell Amy that her Aunt Chloe was one of the most beautiful women he'd seen in a long while but, then, Amy could be relied on not to syphon that information into the hospital gossip network. Neither would she betray the part about Chloe's special magic. Jon couldn't quite put his finger on what kind of magic it was, but he wasn't so far gone that he couldn't recognise it was there.

He sipped his coffee, watching as the nurse busied herself, trying to tell himself that he shouldn't be shaken by any of this. It was straightforward. A housemate for six weeks while he made his own place habitable. A child who needed his help. It was neat and clean and nothing that he couldn't deal with.

Not like his marriage. Jon had often wondered whether the time bomb that had finally blown everything apart had been primed on his and Helen's wedding day. Ticking away the moments of pure happiness, measuring all the times that attention to two blossoming careers had demanded they spend apart, and tallying up each moment of tired indifference. Then exploding suddenly, sending shards of vitriol that scattered themselves across every aspect of Jon's life, embedding themselves deep into his heart.

A heart that had been hardened by time, but now felt under attack. Chloe's house was a long way away from the perfect, magazine-cover home that he and Helen had shared, but he'd found himself suddenly at ease there, as if he'd just pulled on a favourite shirt. Maybe it was a little frayed in places but it was warm and comfortable, fitting him perfectly. And if her house made him yearn for something he didn't have, then Chloe herself turned an obscure ache into an urgent stab of longing.

'Chloe's gone now?' The nurse interrupted his reverie.

'Yeah.'

'So you're left holding the baby…' The nurse bent down, smoothing Amy's brow in a motion of comfort. 'Pretty little thing, isn't she?'

'Yes, she is.' Jon had always assumed that Amy's light auburn curls and the freckles across her nose must be inherited from her father. But some quirk of genetics had rendered the little girl the image of her aunt, right down to her honey-brown eyes.

The feeling that he was being sucked in by Chloe's eyes wasn't an entirely unpleasant one. But he was in control of his life now. He could decide to ignore whatever part of Chloe he wanted to.

'This is the last thing Chloe needs right now. I hope she doesn't overdo things.' The nurse smoothed the blanket over Amy in one of those entirely unnecessary acts of caring that always made Jon proud to be part of a team.

'I heard she'd been ill.'

'Yes. I don't think that any of the doctors down here

could miss a case of Guillain-Barré syndrome if they tried. Chloe made sure of that.'

The thought made Jon smile. Guillain-Barré was enough to deal with on its own, without undertaking an information awareness exercise. But somehow he expected no less of Chloe.

'She shared her experience?'

'You bet she did. Before she could even walk, she persuaded someone to wheel her down here and told the senior houseman that if any of the juniors hadn't seen Guillain-Barré before, she was ready to be examined. It was pretty painful for her, but she sat through it and slurred her way through all of their questions as well.'

'That's...' Suddenly Jon couldn't find the words.

'Beyond the call of duty, I'd say.'

'Yeah. Way beyond...' If Chloe could do that, then backing off now was suddenly unthinkable. Jon put his cup down, ignoring the film-wrapped sandwich. 'Why don't you get on, now? I've everything I need here, and I'll make sure that Amy's all right.'

Chloe had expected to find that Hannah was upset, but the reality had been much worse. Hannah had been sitting in the lounge, her arms wound around her stomach, her face impassive apart from the tears that had trickled down her cheeks. She'd looked almost as if she was in shock, rocking slightly as if to comfort herself.

Chloe had made a cup of tea and they'd talked for a while. Or rather Chloe had done most of the talking, while Hannah had listened disinterestedly, as if the words had meant nothing to her. But Chloe knew she'd got through to Hannah because when she'd suggested that she come and see Amy, to make sure she was all right, Hannah had stood up and put on her jacket.

Jon had left a message with the paediatric A and E receptionist, and Chloe led Hannah up to the children's ward. She could see him, sitting next to Amy's cot, through the large window that divided the ward from the reception area, and when he caught sight of them, he rose.

'How is she?' Hannah's first question for Jon was the one she'd asked Chloe as soon as she'd walked through the door.

'She's doing well. I wanted her admitted to hospital as a precaution, but the antibiotics will clear the UTI and she'll be fine.' His voice was gentle but very firm, as if just saying it was going to make it happen.

'I'm sorry.' There was nothing but dull despair in Hannah's voice.

'There's nothing to be sorry for. You did exactly the right thing for Amy. I wish that some other mothers were as sensible as you.'

Hannah looked up at him. Jon seemed to be making about as much impression on Hannah as Chloe had, but he was trying. And somewhere, on some level, Hannah must be hearing all of this.

'Why don't you come and see her, eh?' Jon picked up Hannah's hand, tucking it into the crook of his arm. He flashed a smile towards Chloe and she nodded. She'd done her best to convince Hannah that she was a good mother and she'd done nothing wrong, but Hannah had just shrugged. *You're my sister, you would say that.* Maybe the words would have greater weight if they came from someone else.

She watched as Jon walked Hannah into the ward, getting her to sit down in the chair that he'd been occupying. He gestured towards the drip, obviously explaining everything that was being done for Amy, and

waited as Hannah slowly reached out to touch Amy's
hand. Then he turned, walking out of the ward to stand
next to Chloe.

'She seems…fragile.' Jon was watching Hannah and
Amy intently.

'Yes, she is.' Chloe looked up at him, but he didn't
return her gaze. 'She's doing a good job of beating herself up over what's happened.'

Jon frowned. 'What *has* happened? As far as I can
see, Hannah thought that there was something wrong
with Amy and did everything she could to get the proper
medical treatment for her.'

If only he would look at her. Chloe could really do
with just a moment in the warmth of his reassurance.
But it seemed that was carefully rationed, and that only
Amy and Hannah were entitled to it.

'When she went to see the doctor, she said that he
looked at Amy and said it was most likely just a virus,
and to call him immediately if she was worried. Hannah started to cry and he asked a lot of questions about
how she was doing. She thinks that the doctor put all of
her worries about Amy down to her own mental state.'

The frown deepened. 'Hannah was crying when I
saw her. *And* she had a sick baby…'

'Yes. Well, that was a few hours later and maybe
Amy's symptoms were a lot more pronounced.' Or
maybe Jon was just a good doctor, who understood
people. 'Apparently Hannah's been to her doctor before, about feeling she can't cope.'

'You knew this?'

That was the bitterest part of it. Hannah had been
in trouble and she hadn't said anything. 'No. Neither
did James.'

'What are you going to do?' He turned suddenly,

and the warmth in his face cut through the feeling that Chloe had failed Hannah yet again. This time, it was all going to be different.

'I've given James a call. He's on holiday in Cornwall, but he's driving back up tonight and he'll stay with Hannah at my place. I'll stay here with Amy, and we can talk in the morning.'

'Sounds like a plan. If there's anything I can do...' He shrugged, as if he couldn't think of what that anything might be. A moment in his arms perhaps. Having him tell her that everything was going to be fine. But that was something that could only be given, not asked for.

'You've done a great deal already. I'm very grateful.' If that sounded a lot like a *thank you and goodbye*, then maybe it was. Relying on other people to help her was only going to lead to disappointment.

'It's nothing. Just paying it forward.' Chloe shot him a querying look. 'James was very good to me when my marriage broke up, he put me up until I found a place of my own. That was when I got to know Hannah.'

'I'm sorry, I didn't realise—'

'It's water under the bridge now.' The downward quirk of his lips told Chloe that even if it was, it was something that still pained him. 'From what James tells me, you were dealing with your own problems at that time. I've only ever come across one case of Guillain-Barré syndrome but I know it's a tough journey to take.'

It *had* been tough, suddenly losing any sensation other than pain in both legs and one arm, contending with the real fear that the accompanying paralysis might keep spreading until it reached her chest and the other side of her face.

'That's water under the bridge, too.'

Suddenly he was looking at her again, his face suffused with all the warmth that he'd offered to Amy and Hannah. 'You're sure about that. Because if you can't cope...'

'I *can* cope.' The words were defensive on her lips. 'Sorry.'

'No... I'm sorry, I didn't mean to snap.' It wasn't Jon's fault that few of the promises that had been made around her hospital bed had come to fruition. That both Jake and her best friend had sworn they'd stand by her through this, and they'd ended up standing by each other.

Chloe took a deep breath, trying to puff out the echoes of the lonely despair she'd felt when she'd realised that her partner and her friend were now an item and that neither of them had the guts to come and tell her. This wasn't the time to be raking over old memories because she had to think about the challenges of the present.

'Look, I... I couldn't give Hannah the support she needed when I was ill. I can now.'

He nodded. 'And that's important to you.'

'Yes, it is. Hannah's not had an easy time, she was so young when our parents died. James and I tried to help her through it, but we were both at university and neither of us were in a position to give her a stable home. My mother's sister fostered her, and... Aunt Sylvie's very kind, very loving, but Hannah always wanted to live with me. When she was fifteen I took her.'

'But you fell ill?'

'Yes, and Hannah went to live with James. I don't think she really understood why I wouldn't keep her. She told me that she'd help look after me, but I didn't want to make her into my carer. She deserved more than that.'

The frank approval in his eyes meant a lot more than it should. Chloe had wanted his understanding, craved his warmth, and now that she had it, it was too much to bear. She looked away, staring at Hannah and Amy.

'Hannah was almost sixteen when she ran away. I couldn't help look for her, I could hardly manage to get out of the house. It was James who found her and brought her back, and he was the one who looked after her when she realised that she was pregnant.'

'And you think you let Hannah down?' His tone suggested that Jon thought quite the opposite, but Chloe begged to differ.

'I think that Hannah and Amy need me right now. And that I'm going to be there for both of them.' It was too late to save Hannah from the turbulence of her teenage years, but she would find a way to put things right now. Because this time it wasn't only a matter of saving Hannah, it was a matter of saving Amy, too.

CHAPTER THREE

IT HAD BEEN a restless night, sleeping in the folding bed next to Amy's cot, and so far the morning hadn't been much easier. Chloe hadn't seen Jon when she'd returned home to talk to Hannah and James, and she'd assumed that he'd escaped over to his place when his shift had ended this morning.

But when she got back to the hospital he was there, sitting in the chair next to Amy's cot with Amy on his lap, talking to her and gently stopping her from grabbing at the bandage on her arm that covered the cannula.

'She's a lot better this morning.' One of the nurses had stopped at Chloe's side, and Chloe dragged her gaze away from Jon. Each time she saw him with Amy it was impossible not to notice that someone so strong could be so gentle.

'Does he usually check up on his patients like this?'

The nurse grinned. 'He's no stranger up here, he often pops in to see how the children he's had admitted are doing. He seems to have taken a bit of a shine to Amy, though.'

It seemed that he had. And Amy had clearly taken a bit of a shine to Jon, looking up at him, her hand reaching to touch his face.

But Chloe was here now. And she could cope. Thanking the nurse, she walked into the ward.

'Good morning.' Jon had been so bound up with Amy that he'd failed to register Chloe's approach until she'd spoken.

He made to deliver Amy into her arms, and the little girl started to cry, clinging on to him. Jon pulled an embarrassed face, which didn't quite conceal his pleasure at Amy being so determined not to let him go, and Chloe motioned for him to stay as he was.

'How are things?' He took a moment out from Amy to ask the question.

'We're getting there. I think…' Chloe took her jacket off and sat down. 'James is taking Hannah back down to Cornwall with him, and I'm going to look after Amy for a while.'

His attention was suddenly all hers. 'She doesn't want to stay here?'

'She's…' Chloe shrugged. 'She's got it into her head that I can look after Amy better than she can. Maybe that's true for the moment. Hannah definitely needs a break so she can think things through.'

'And when she has?' Concern was etched deep into his face.

'When she has, she'll see that she's a great mother and that James and I are both here for her to give her all the support she needs to make a good life for herself and for Amy.'

'Sounds good to me.'

'You don't seem very convinced.' He obviously knew as well as Chloe did that things probably weren't going to be as easy as that.

He shrugged. 'I'm…not really the one to ask about families.'

'You mean the kids are a lot less complicated?'

'Now you mention it…' Amy grabbed at his nose and he gave her a look of exaggerated shock. Then he pinched her nose, putting his thumb between his fingers as he pulled his hand away and showing it to Amy.

'Mine…!' Amy reached for his hand.

'That's your nose, is it?' Jon wiggled his thumb and Amy nodded.

It was almost painful to watch. All the support and love that anyone could want, and which Chloe couldn't bring herself to trust in. But Jon had just said it himself. Something had persuaded him that families weren't his strong point, and for him it was all about the children.

He was busy replacing Amy's nose and threading an imaginary needle to stitch it back on again while Amy held it in place. 'How's that, then? Let Auntie Chloe have a look, see if I've got it straight.'

'It's straight…' Suddenly the game seemed too good to end it here. Chloe clapped her hand theatrically over her mouth. 'Call yourself a doctor? Amy…he's put your nose back on upside down!'

Amy pulled at her nose, inspecting her empty hand, and Jon laughed.

'Look, this is the way you do it… Perhaps Auntie Chloe can do a better job putting it back on again.' A flash of his blue eyes, full of intoxicating fun. 'She's obviously the expert around here.'

The make-believe needle and thread was handed over to Chloe, and she pulled her chair a little closer. Amy held her nose on, giggling, while Chloe pretended to sew it back, her knees almost touching Jon's. When he leaned over to gently untangle the drip attached to Amy's arm, his fingers brushed hers, making her shiver.

'Perfect.' Jon inspected her handiwork, then dropped

a kiss onto his finger, planting it on Amy's nose then lifting the little girl onto Chloe's lap.

'Are you okay here?' He pulled his chair back, as if he knew that suddenly he'd got altogether too close. 'What about Amy's things?'

'James is dealing with that. He's taking Hannah back to her place to pack and then he'll drop Amy's things back at my place and take Hannah on down to Cornwall.'

Jon nodded. 'I guess Cornwall's not so far. If Hannah needs to come back.'

'Yes.' Chloe sighed. 'I hate them being apart but… Hannah seems to need some time at the moment. And some sleep as well.'

'Yeah. I can identify with that.' He rubbed one hand across his face, seeming suddenly drawn.

'Why don't you go home and get some rest? James and Hannah will be gone by now and I'll give them a call and tell them not to wake you up when they get back with Amy's things.'

'You want anything before I go? Something to eat?'

'No, I've eaten. Go.'

Amy seemed to have run out of energy too, and Chloe felt her snuggle against her, refusing to wake up and wave goodbye to Jon. He grinned, brushing Amy's cheek with his finger, and Chloe watched his back as he walked away.

He turned for one final wave through the window from the lobby outside. Even distance, even the glass couldn't dim the bright blue of his tired eyes and Chloe wished that he wasn't leaving her behind.

It was the first step on a long and slippery slope. A look, a shared smile that would catapult her into neediness and leave her in a tangled heap on the floor when

Jon went his own way. However much she liked his smile, it just wasn't worth it.

Amy started to fret in her arms and Chloe leaned down to comfort her. 'It's going to be okay, Amy. Everything's going to be okay, you'll see.'

Jon hadn't thought that a battered teddy bear and a bar of chocolate could possibly be such controversial items. He'd selected the teddy bear from the bag of toys that James had left in the hall while he'd slept, reckoning that the most worn was probably the most loved. And the chocolate was the same seventy per cent cocoa blend that he'd found stashed away at the back of one of the kitchen cabinets.

But when he'd gone to the children's ward that evening, Chloe had looked at them both as if they were poisoned. She propped the teddy bear up in Amy's cot, leaving the chocolate untouched on the locker.

'Isn't your shift about to start?' It was a clear invitation for him to go, even if he'd only just arrived. He probably should go, but something stopped him. Maybe the fact that no one in their right mind refused a visitor when they were in hospital, and that Chloe's attitude betrayed some other worry.

'Not for another hour.' He drew up a chair and sat down. He could probably find somewhere else to be, but sleep had rearranged his muddled thoughts, and on waking the decision had seemed obvious. Chloe needed help, and he was there to give it.

She hesitated. She looked different tonight, softer, dressed in a pair of casual trousers with a top that he reckoned was supposed to slide from one shoulder to reveal the strap of a cotton vest underneath. The warmth in here had touched her cheeks with pink, and her hair curled loosely around her face in what seemed like an invitation to touch.

Clearly that invitation wasn't extended to him. And even if it had been, Jon had no intention of taking it up. The decision on that point had been clear, too. Help out, but don't touch.

'You don't need to do this.' She pressed her lips together, and they too became a little pinker. Jon wondered whether they tasted pink, and dismissed the thought with no more than a moment's regret.

'Do what?'

'You know…' A small, delicious frown indicated that Chloe understood quite well that he was going to make her explain. 'We all really appreciate what you did yesterday, Jon. But you don't have to feel responsible for us, just because… You have other things to be getting on with.'

For a moment he couldn't imagine what those other things might be. Chloe and Amy seemed more important than anything.

'My house, you mean?'

'Yes. And your job.'

'I imagine the builders will be quite pleased to find that I haven't been interfering with things over the weekend. And my job doesn't require twenty-four-hour input.'

'All the same…' She shrugged. 'Amy and I are fine, really. We're not your problem.'

He was beginning to feel that they were—which was a problem in itself. But Jon could handle it.

'I can help, can't I? It's never easy, taking responsibility for a sick child.'

'No, but I can manage. You don't need to keep popping in to see if we're all right.'

Leaning forward, he picked up the chocolate, unwrapping one end and breaking off a piece. 'Okay. I get it. You're managing.'

The look on her face, when he started to eat, was a classic. Clearly she had reckoned on saving the chocolate and eating it when he was safely out of the way. He hesitated for a moment before he popped a second piece into his mouth and she broke suddenly.

'You're eating my chocolate.'

Jon grinned, as innocently as he could manage. 'Yeah. Since you're managing so well, I thought you wouldn't want it.'

She seemed on the cusp of either smiling or sulking. Chloe went for the smile. 'That's different. Don't you know that some people have a special relationship with chocolate?'

That was exactly what he'd been banking on. Jon handed her the bar and she broke a piece off. 'So I'm allowed to bring you chocolate, then?'

She twisted her mouth, obviously willing to accept that she was beaten. 'Yes. You're allowed to bring me chocolate.'

'And Amy her bear?' He glanced over to where Amy was subjecting the bear to her own version of nursing care, shoving it under the blanket of her cot.

'Yes, that was a kind thought. Papa Bear's her favourite.' She smiled at Amy, who ignored her, in favour of banging Papa Bear on the nose, presumably in an attempt to make him go to sleep.

'She seems much better.'

'Yes, she is. She's stopped clinging to me and wanting to be held. They should be letting her go on Monday when the tests come back.'

Chloe turned her gaze back onto Jon. 'Look, I'm

sorry if I seemed ungrateful. When I was ill… You get to understand who you can really rely on at times like that.'

'Yourself?' It wasn't a universal experience. Many—most—people were comforted by the support of those around them when they became gravely ill.

'Yes, myself. James did the best he could, but he had Carol and the kids *and* Hannah to worry about.'

'So you told him that you were fine and that you didn't need anything.' Which was exactly what Chloe was telling him now. Jon's determination to take that with a pinch of salt strengthened.

She shrugged. 'I might have intimated something of the sort.'

'And since you're a doctor, and James probably wouldn't have heard of Guillain-Barré syndrome, he'd have just taken your word for it.'

'Well, he looked it up on the internet. But the internet can be wrong sometimes.' Chloe fixed Jon with a glare. 'And you're not telling him any different now.'

'What you choose to tell anyone about your illness is none of my business.' James would be horrified if he knew what Jon suspected, that Chloe had been incapacitated and coping alone for a long time after she'd been released from hospital. But there was no point in telling him that now.

'Thank you.'

It was obvious why Chloe had been reluctant to rely on her brother, but it was rather more of a puzzle why she'd applied the same principle to everyone. And why she seemed so intent on applying it again now. But that wasn't his business either. As long as she accepted that she could at least tell him if she needed something, they'd get along just fine. He took the small lint bandage that he'd found in the kitchen drawer out of his pocket.

'Hey, Amy.' The little girl turned to look at him. 'Is Papa Bear ill?'

'Yes.' Amy nodded gravely.

'Right. Shall we see if we can make him better?' It wasn't unusual for children to transfer what was going on in their heads onto their toys, and making the battered bear better would help Amy too.

Chloe caught onto the idea and grinned. 'Do you think he needs a bandage?' She leaned over, lifting Amy out of the cot and onto her lap, and Jon reached for the bear.

'Poor Papa Bear. Make him better.' Amy turned her trusting eyes on him.

'All right, Nurse Amy. You hold him, and I'll just put this bandage on his arm.' Jon nodded to the dressing on Amy's arm, which protected the cannula. 'Just like yours.'

Amy nodded, and Chloe kissed the top of her niece's head. 'See Amy. Doctor Jon's going to make him better.'

It was a start, at least. If Chloe didn't trust him enough to take anything for herself, she was much more comfortable with taking all she could get for Amy. And Jon was sure of his ground. He'd be in and then out again, a clean operation, carried out with all the precision that his medical training had taught him to apply. It was perfectly possible to help the sister of a good friend out without doing anything stupid like falling in love with her.

CHAPTER FOUR

CHLOE WASN'T ABOUT to admit that she'd overreacted. It might have looked that way to Jon, but he clearly hadn't learned yet that even the best of friends would choose their own agenda when it came to the crunch.

That actually wasn't the problem. The problem was that every time she saw him she wanted to hold onto him, to make him stay. Wanted him to prove that Jake had been mistaken.

Not that she cared all that much about what Jake thought, or did, any more. He'd left her because he'd been unable to see past her illness, and wouldn't believe that she could make a full recovery, and she'd shown that he was wrong on that score. But she was human, and wanting to be touched by a man was natural. Wanting to show herself that her body could be a source of pleasure and not pain…that was natural enough, too.

But Jon wasn't the one to prove that point with. If she touched him, and let him touch her, she wouldn't want to let him go.

What he said made sense, though. Chloe was dreading talking to her supervisor on Monday and telling him that she had a sick baby to look after. He'd been so understanding over the Guillain-Barré, taking her back in her old job and letting her work part time for as long as she'd needed to. Everyone's patience ran out sooner or later, and hopefully this wasn't going to be the last straw. If it turned out that she would have to look after Amy for longer than the next two weeks, she was going to need all the help she could get.

A restless night did little to quell her worries, but a new arrival in the ward early on Sunday morning put them into perspective—a little boy of around three, a breathing mask over his face, who lay surrounded by monitoring equipment.

'What's the matter with him?' she whispered to the nurse who was with him.

'Smoke inhalation.' The nurses all knew that Chloe was a doctor, and were more frank with her than with the other parents on the ward.

'Where are his parents?'

'Dad's on the burns unit. I think Mum's still down in A and E.'

'Shall I go down and see if I can find her? She must be worried sick.'

'I think… Yeah, I think that's her now.' The nurse grinned. 'With Amy's favourite doctor.'

There was no question about who that was. Chloe looked up and saw Jon pushing a woman in a wheelchair into the lobby. She was wearing a hospital gown and a nasal cannula indicated that there was probably an oxygen cylinder tucked under the blanket over her knees. Chloe left the nurse with the boy and went outside to meet them.

Jon was looking around, trying to catch the attention of one of the nurses but they were all busy. When he saw Chloe he spoke to the woman.

'Ah. Here's someone who might know…' He turned

his blue eyes up to meet hers. 'There's a little boy, three years old. He's just been admitted.'

'Through here.' Chloe indicated the ward, and Jon nodded a thank-you, wheeling the woman through.

'Nicky…' The woman's voice was hoarse and cracked. She stretched out her hand towards the boy in the bed and tried to get out of the wheelchair but Jon laid his hand on her shoulder, stopping her.

'Stay there, Kathy. He's all right.'

'His hands…' Kathy wouldn't stop reaching, and Chloe saw that one of Nicky's hands was still blackened by smoke.

'It's all right. His hands aren't burned, I cleaned him up and checked. He must have picked that bit of soot up when I took his pyjamas off.' Jon's reassurance calmed Kathy a little.

'He's not burned at all?'

'Nothing. Your husband did a good job, Kathy, he got him out of the house without a scratch on him. It's just the smoke inhalation. We need to watch him carefully for a little while, just the same as we need to watch you.'

'I'm all right.' Kathy didn't take her eyes off her son.

'Well, we need to make sure. I sprang you out of observation on the strict condition that I made sure you stayed in the chair and breathed through your nose. You're not getting the full benefit of the oxygen if you breathe through your mouth.'

Jon gave Kathy a look of gentle reproof and she closed her mouth, her chest moving as she took a deep breath through her nose.

'Better. Thank you.' Jon grinned at her and she managed a smile. Chloe stepped forward, taking Kathy's hand.

'I'm Chloe. That's my niece over there, but I'm a

doctor too. Would you like me to clean Nicky's hand?' It made little difference whether the boy's hand was clean or dirty at the moment, but it was all that Chloe could think of to make Kathy feel better.

Kathy nodded, giving her a tight smile.

Chloe fetched some warm water and carefully wiped and dried Nicky's hand. Jon had stepped away from them and was talking quietly on his phone, and Chloe pushed the wheelchair a little closer to the bed so that Kathy could touch her son.

'Is there anyone we can call for you? A friend or relative?'

'Dr Lambert's calling my sister. He's so kind…' A tear rolled down Kathy's cheek.

'Yes, he is. He's a very good doctor as well, and Nicky's in good hands here.' Chloe put her arm around Kathy's shoulders. 'Don't cry, now. Just breathe.'

Jon was still on the phone, talking intently. He saw Chloe watching him, and before she could avert her eyes he flashed her a smile and ended the call.

'Your sister's coming, she'll be here in an hour. She's going to get the children to school and then come straight here.' He bent down, squatting on his heels in front of Kathy. 'I called down to see how your husband's doing—'

'Is he all right?' Kathy's hand flew to her mouth.

'He's comfortable and in no danger. He needs care, he has smoke inhalation and burns to his arm, but they'll heal.'

'Thank you… Thank you…'

That smile again. The one that would have calmed a charging rhino. Or made a stone feel something. 'I hear your husband was a hero.'

Tears rolled down Kathy's cheeks. 'He told me to

go downstairs. He went to fetch Nicky and rolled him up in a blanket...'

'The doctor said that you could see him for ten minutes. I can take you down, and bring you straight back here to be with Nicky.'

Kathy's gaze moved to her son and then back to Jon, in a dilemma. Nicky was lying quietly at the moment, but he was going to need his mother's comfort when the trauma of the last few hours started to sink in.

'Will you let me watch Nicky for you while you're gone? I'll call you if there's any change or if he becomes distressed.' Chloe spoke up.

'Would you...?' Kathy was still uncertain.

'I'll stay right here, by his bed. I can call Jon, and he'll bring you straight back here.'

Jon nodded, taking his phone from the trouser pocket of his scrubs and putting it in Kathy's hand. 'Here. Hang onto it for me.'

Kathy nodded. 'I'd like to see him. I want to tell him—'

Jon got to his feet, smiling. 'He'll be wanting to hear it. And Chloe will keep a good eye on Nicky. If we all share the load, we can cover everything.'

Chloe had been wondering whether that last comment had been aimed at her. Jon's glance had flipped momentarily towards her when he'd said it, and she'd pretended not to notice.

He took Kathy away, and brought her back again twenty minutes later. Even though his shift had ended almost an hour ago, he waited until Kathy's sister arrived, taking ten minutes to change out of his scrubs and then returning to the ward. This time Chloe couldn't help a little thrill of excitement because he was quite obviously here just for her.

'Breakfast?'

'Shouldn't you be getting home for some sleep?' Her treacherous heart hoped that he wouldn't go.

'I'm not quite tired enough yet.'

They left Amy playing quietly and walked down to the canteen. Jon piled a plate full of all the breakfast items on the menu and Chloe rummaged in her hand-bag for the small sachet of teabags.

'Hot water? Or can I tempt you to something else?' He gestured towards the pile of flapjacks.

'No, that's okay. I'll watch you eat.'

They found a table in a quiet corner and Jon attacked his food like a man who hadn't eaten in the last week. She waited until he slowed a little, sipping her tea.

'So how's Kathy's husband?'

'Second- and third-degree burns on the top of his arm and shoulder. He could well need skin grafts.'

'But he'll be okay.'

'Yes. Apparently he was pretty lucky to escape with just that.'

'He knew Kathy was there?'

Jon's face broke into a smile. 'He was drowsy from the pain relief but he knew all right. Brave man.'

'Going to fetch Nicky like that.'

'Yes. And the way he told Kathy that it all looked worse than it felt, and that she wasn't to worry about him. He was okay, and she should stay with Nicky.'

He paused for a moment, looking at Chloe, and then started to eat again. She wondered whether *that* comment was aimed at her as well. If it was, she didn't deserve the kind of respect that Kathy's husband did. She'd just done what she'd had to do, when she'd sent Hannah away to live with James.

'I'll go down there later. If he can't have visitors, I can at least take a message from Kathy. Let him know how she and Nicky are doing.'

'That's nice. I'm sure he'd appreciate it.'

He finished the last few mouthfuls from his plate and leaned back in his seat with a satisfied sigh. Then he turned to the toast.

'I've been thinking…'

Chloe asked the question that he was clearly waiting for. 'What about?'

'What are you going to do when Amy comes out of hospital?'

'I'll take some time off work. She should be coming out on Monday but it won't be until the afternoon so I'll speak to my head of department in the morning. When she's fully well, I'll make enquiries about getting her into the hospital crèche.'

He nodded. 'I could look after her next week.'

'You can't work nights and look after a baby all day. You're not *that* superhuman.'

'Ah, so you think I'm just a bit superhuman…' Jon grinned at her. 'But, no, I wasn't thinking of doing that. The guy I'm covering for is back from sick leave next week. I'm working on Monday night, but I'm not needed again until the following Sunday. After that I've got some more time off arranged before I start work permanently, and I can use that to work on the house.'

It was tempting. Very tempting, in more ways than just the practical. Chloe stared at him, trying to frame a polite but firm refusal.

'What?' He didn't wait for her answer. 'Come on,

you know Amy will be safe with me. And a week off
with her might be relaxing.'

'You think so?'

Jon shrugged. 'Well, a change is as good as a rest.
Amy can't frame a sensible sentence about either medi-
cine *or* building materials.'

He seemed so sure. And although it was difficult
to fault his logic, his absolute commitment to the idea
didn't make any sense.

'This is my responsibility, Jon. Why won't you take
no for an answer?'

It was a fair enough question. If he were in Chloe's
shoes, he'd be asking the same thing. Avoiding her like
the plague and then suddenly jumping in with both feet
might not be a very good basis for trust, but he'd just
have to use a bit of persuasion.

'When do you think Hannah's going to be able to
take full-time responsibility for Amy?' He avoided the
question with one of his own.

She sighed. 'I spoke with James last night. We both
agreed to take things slowly.'

'Then you're going to need to pace yourself. Save
your leave for when you really need it.'

'That's true, and it's a very good point. You haven't
answered my question, though.'

So he wasn't getting off the hook that easily. 'Families are important.'

'That's true too.' She was circling the rim of her
empty cup with her finger. Jon could practically hear
the next question forming and he didn't want to answer
that one either.

'Look, James will tell you that I'm not close to my

family. I speak with my sister regularly, once a fort-night. I mark it in my diary to remind me.'

She looked up at him thoughtfully, obviously trying to comprehend an arrangement that was so different from the way she kept in touch with James and Hannah, just picking up the phone whenever she had something to say. Never needing to remember to do it, because her brother and sister were a part of her life.

'Do you say much?'

'Yeah, we say quite a bit. We've learned not to say anything that really matters, because that's likely to get us into trouble. It's a long story. But you and James and Hannah...you have something special. It's worth taking care of.'

'When our parents died, all we had was each other.' She pointed to his empty cup. 'Do you want a refill?'

'There's still another cup in the pot.' Jon picked up the small, stainless-steel coffee pot and poured the rest of its contents into his cup. 'Am I going to need this?'

'I'm not sure. You said it was a long story.'

Suddenly he wanted everything out in the open. He wanted to let Chloe know where he stood, and then they could forget about these games and get on with the practical.

'Right...' Jon wondered where to start, and decided that the very beginning was probably best. 'Well...boy meets girl, I guess...'

Her eyes widened suddenly. For one delicious moment Jon let the misunderstanding hang in the air between them.

'I met my ex-wife at the Freshers' Ball at medical school.'

'Ah. Yes, of course.' She found another teabag from the seemingly endless supply in her bag and put it into her cup, splashing hot water onto it. 'And…then you got married?'

'Yes, we did, after we'd both qualified. Everyone pretty much expected we would, we had the same interests, the same goals in life…our families got on so well that Helen's parents and mine used to go on weekend breaks together.'

Chloe's hand flew to her mouth, stifling the inevitable comment. Jon couldn't help smiling, even though there wasn't a great deal to smile about in all of this.

'Yeah, I know. When the in-laws start planning Christmas together there's a certain amount of expectation involved. But we didn't let them down, we got a nice house together, both of us had good jobs that we loved. We were very happy.'

Chloe didn't look convinced about any of this. Maybe she was smarter than he'd been. He'd thought then that love was something he could catch and keep, but now he knew better.

'I got a promotion, and Helen started working nights. We saw less and less of each other, and when we did there were more and more arguments. We became like strangers living in the same house.'

Even now, the quiet hopelessness, the feeling that if this was all there was to life it had somehow fallen short of what he'd wanted, reverberated through Jon's heart. He'd never smelled Helen's soap, the way he had Chloe's. Never checked the sell-by dates of her food in the fridge. Maybe if he had, things would have been different, but it was too late to think about that now.

'In the end, Helen asked me to leave. When we told our families that we were splitting up, the crash of broken expectations was deafening. Everyone was looking for a reason, why the perfect marriage should no longer be so perfect, and I couldn't give them one. My parents talked to Helen's, and then came to me and demanded to know whether I'd had an affair. I hadn't...'

'And you set them straight?' It was warming to find that Chloe's first reaction was one of belief, and not the disbelief that his parents had voiced.

'I tried to.' Jon shrugged. 'They were always very fond of Helen, though. And she was ready to believe anything that anyone said about me at that point. The whole thing blew up in our faces and became very bitter. Helen's solicitor drew up the divorce papers, and when I got them they cited adultery.'

'But...if that wasn't true...' Chloe's brow was creased with thought. 'I mean, they're legal papers. Wouldn't they be null and void? You'd still be married.'

Maybe it was the odd twist of logic. Or maybe just that Chloe was basing that logic on such an unquestioning belief. Jon couldn't help laughing.

'I've no idea. I wouldn't sign them, I held out for irreconcilable differences. There was no doubt at all about that one. My mother was furious with me, and that was when James came to the rescue and offered me a place to stay. I moved out of my parents' house...'

He shrugged. The softness in Chloe's eyes said all that there was left to say. The stupid, needless conflict, which had broken his family apart and driven him away because he'd been unable to handle all the back-biting.

'So, you see, I know how easily families can break. And I know how hard you and James have fought for yours and that's special. Call it meddling, but if I can help you now...'

He didn't know what he was hoping for. Maybe Chloe did. Jon reached forward, taking her hand, curling his fingers around hers.

'If you can help me now, it won't make anything right for you.'

Jon was used to people taking his help without question. Without even thinking about what it might mean to him. That was okay, it was his job and it was what he'd chosen to do, but Chloe… Chloe was different from anyone he'd ever met, and each time she showed that, it touched him.

'I know. I'm past caring about that now, and I concentrate on what I'm good at, my job and my friendships. I've given up on everything else, but you won't give up on Hannah, and that means something.'

Suddenly she looked up at him, her eyes as soft as honey. 'So…do you really think you're prepared for this? Amy can be quite a handful.'

'I doubt it, but I'll give it a go. What can go wrong?'

She smiled suddenly. 'I don't know. I dare say Amy will come up with something.'

CHAPTER FIVE

IN A WORLD full of imperfect relationships, Jon had bucked the trend and got himself something perfect. And it had broken and then descended into a chaos of hard feelings and lies. No wonder he didn't want to go back there again.

And that suited Chloe. Promises to stay for ever hadn't meant much when her parents had died, and even less when Jake had left. Even Hannah couldn't stay with Amy right now. But Jon had made it clear that there was a limit to what he could promise, and that was oddly reassuring.

But the silence in the house when she opened the front door wasn't. Amy had been released from hospital on Monday, and when Jon had got home from work on Tuesday morning, Chloe had left her niece in his care. She'd resisted the temptation to phone him any more than a couple of times during the day to ask if everything was all right, and left work at five-thirty on the dot.

She closed the front door. Maybe he'd taken Amy out for a while. But the car seat was still in the hall. Chloe walked into the sitting room and found Jon sprawled on the sofa, with Amy lying fast asleep on his chest.

It was odd, but every time she saw him he seemed a

little more deliciously handsome. Perhaps it was Amy's tiny hands, clutching at his shirt as she slept, his own arms providing a safe enclosure for her. Who could resist that?

Amy stirred and he opened his eyes immediately, his hand moving to spread protectively across her back. Then he caught sight of Chloe and she stepped back instinctively, aware that she'd been caught watching him.

'Hi…' She smiled foolishly as he sat up, bringing Amy with him. 'Good day?'

'Yeah.' He surveyed the toys, scattered across the floor. 'I'm afraid I didn't get much time to tidy up, though…'

'Amy's okay?'

'Yes, she's been fine.'

Chloe grinned. 'That's your mission for the day sorted, then.' She picked up a few of the toys, piling them up in the corner of the room, and then sat down next to him.

'How was your day?'

'Good.' She leaned over towards Amy, who was waking up in his arms. 'I missed you, Amy.'

Amy wriggled round, reaching for Chloe. 'Beautiful Auntie Chloe…'

Amy enunciated the words perfectly. Something she'd heard, maybe, and was mimicking…?

No. They were just words. Probably jumbled together without any particular meaning. Amy was beginning to do that, mixing the baby talk with the odd word that sounded as if it had some thought behind it, but generally didn't.

Jon looked as startled as she was. 'I…wonder where she picked that up from.'

'So I'm *not* beautiful?' Teasing him wasn't a bad way to cover her own discomfiture.

Jon narrowed his eyes. 'I'm a little too tired to come up with an answer that's not going to incriminate me.'

So maybe Amy *had* heard it from him. If so, it was probably best not to enquire. She took Amy from him, hugging her. 'So what did you get up to today?'

'We went to the park. There's a great playground...' He grinned. 'Amy enjoyed it too.'

'She didn't give you a chance to sleep?' Jon had reassembled Amy's cot, and it stood next to the sofa.

'She slept. I reckoned I might sleep, but...' He shrugged. 'I ended up watching her.'

'Just to make sure her dreams were good ones.' Chloe had done exactly the same when she'd been with Amy at the hospital. Hours when she could have been sleeping had somehow turned into hours watching Amy sleep.

'Yeah. I'll get an early night tonight. If I drop off before about nine o'clock perhaps you'll give me a good shake and wake me up.'

A good shake or just the flutter of a child, sleeping on his chest. It seemed that either would be equally as effective. 'How does the smell of coffee work?'

Jon nodded. 'Every time.'

She'd brought him coffee and then disappeared upstairs, taking Amy with her. The transformation between work, the plain blouse and skirt, which weren't plain at all when draped around Chloe's curves, and the casual trousers and tops she wore at home took place out of sight, but that didn't mean that Jon was unaware of it. Just thinking about it woke him up more effectively than if she'd flattened him with a steamroller.

He sat for a while, listening to her moving around

in the kitchen. She was singing, and he heard Amy's voice joining in with hers. He collected the rest of the toys off the floor, adding them to the pile, and wondered whether he should get a proper toy box. Perhaps not. Today might have felt like a new venture, but it was too temporary to warrant anything as solid as the wooden toy box he'd seen in the window of the furniture shop by the park gates.

The smell of cooking drew him into the kitchen. Chloe was chopping tomatoes to add to a bowl of salad, and he could see a large dish of lasagne in the oven. Amy held out her arms to him and instead of just smiling at her and getting on with his job, the way he did with the children at the hospital, picking her up seemed suddenly as if it *was* his job.

'Again…'

'Again?' He raised his eyebrows. 'Again what? I haven't done anything yet.'

The logic was lost on Amy. 'Again!'

'Ah. You mean this?' He swung her up above his head and the little girl laughed with delight.

'You've done it now.' Chloe's face was bright as she looked up from the chopping board.

'Yeah. She kept this up for half an hour this morning.'

'And then she was sick on your head?' Chloe shared the joke with the tomato in front of her, slicing it decisively. Jon swung Amy up one more time then sat down with her on his lap before she could stop squirming and laughing long enough to get out the dreaded word.

'No. I managed to avoid that indignity.' Amy hiccupped, and he jiggled her gently and rubbed her stomach.

Chloe turned. 'You want me to take her?'

That was usually the way. A child got hiccups and either their parents or one of the nurses dealt with it. His job was to deal with the rather more serious issues.

Amy hiccupped again, scrunching her face up. At the moment this seemed just as serious, but rather more difficult to deal with than any medical problem. Living with a child was different from treating them. For one thing, he didn't get so many breaks.

'No, that's okay. Amy and I will deal with this.'

Amy had been fed, and they'd eaten. Jon had taken the cot upstairs, and Chloe had bathed Amy and put her down to sleep. He opened his eyes, after dozing on the sofa, to find her standing in the doorway.

'Do you think if I sit down she'll start crying?'

He smiled. 'Maybe. Would you like a cup of tea?' Suddenly it was as if the one thing he'd tried to avoid, becoming a part of the household and living here instead of just sleeping here, had become a reality. It wasn't as bad as he'd thought it might be.

Chloe nodded. 'Yes, thanks.'

She followed him into the kitchen, sitting down at the table while he made the tea. 'Do you mind my asking? About the Guillain-Barré...?'

'You mean am I feeling tired yet?' She grinned, saving him the awkwardness of working his way onto the question that had been bothering Jon for much of the day.

'Yeah. The last few days have been a break in your routine.' She must have been worried about Amy, and Hannah. And she can't have had a great deal of sleep next to Amy's cot at the hospital.

'I'm okay. I still have a few after-effects, but they haven't got any worse.' Jon shot her a querying look

and she grinned. 'Don't worry. I'm not keeping quiet
about anything.'

'Okay. Just as a matter of interest, what *are* the after-effects?' He put her tea down in front of her and
sat down.

'Sometimes my toes tingle a bit, or the bottom of
my foot feels a little numb. But I've been pretty lucky
on the whole, and I don't get any pain.' She leaned forward towards him. 'Go on. You can ask whatever you
like. It's actually a good thing if doctors know a bit
more about it.'

He took her at her word. 'So what caused it?'

'I had campylobacter. I'd got over that, and had gone
back to work and then…' She shrugged, taking a sip
of her tea.

One of the more common triggers for a rare disease.
Guillain-Barré Syndrome was a result of the immune
system being triggered by a viral infection and attack-
ing the nerves. First a tingling in the hands and feet,
which could spread throughout the whole body, caus-
ing weakness, paralysis and pain.

'I had a fall at work. Lucky really, because there
were a lot of doctors on hand and someone recognised
the symptoms and called in a neurologist. He ordered
an EMG test and before I know it I was in the neuro
ward, with about a thousand medical students hanging
around, taking furious notes.'

'I heard you made the best of your audience.'

Her eyebrows shot up. 'You've been talking about
me behind my back, have you?'

'No, one of the nurses in A and E mentioned it. I've
been listening to other people talking about you behind your back.'

'I suppose I did give them a very full list of my

symptoms, so they'd recognise them if they saw them again. My right arm and my legs were completely paralysed for some weeks, but I could still talk if I put my mind to it.' Jon saw a trace of mischief in her smile and almost choked on his drink. She was indomitable.

'They say doctors make the worst patients.'

'I was a very good patient. I did exactly as I was told, and tried to smile at everyone, which isn't all that easy when one side of your face is paralysed. Dr Malik used to say that he didn't need to explain much to his students, he just sent them to me.' She took another sip of her tea. 'I think he was humouring me.'

Chloe was fingering the gold chain at her neck, absently winding it around her finger. She always seemed to wear it, and what hung on it must be of some special significance to her because it was usually hidden inside her clothes. But he could see now that it was a yellowish crystal.

'Did humouring you work?'

'Lots of things work. Intravenous immunoglobulin for starters. Good food, plenty of sleep. The kindness of strangers...'

'Herbal tea and crystals?' Jon had seen the crystals on the mantelpiece in the sitting room but hadn't realised that Chloe wore one as well. It surprised him that a doctor should put any store in such things.

'Who knows? Not being able to move isn't just something that affects your body.' She shrugged. It seemed that was where Chloe drew the line. She talked about the physical aspects of her illness freely enough, but Jon knew that the emotional ones could be just as devastating and she kept those to herself.

But he'd have to wonder about that later. He was

so tired now that whatever conclusion he came to was bound to be the wrong one.

'I really should turn in…' He looked at his watch. It was almost nine o' clock.

She grinned. 'Will you sleep? After a cup of coffee?'

'I needed the coffee to get me up the stairs. I'll sleep.'

It was odd that Chloe should note that the house had been quiet for the last hour, because generally it *was* quiet. But this was a different kind of quiet, one that seemed to curl around everyone in the house, both sleeping and awake.

She heard a whimpering cry from her bedroom and hurried upstairs. For all Jon's assertions that he could sleep through Armageddon, he'd already proved that a child's crying was enough to wake him, and Chloe picked Amy up from her cot, soothing her.

'All right, sweetie. Mummy can't be here right now, but she'll be back soon. You'll see.' Amy might not fully understand the words, and almost certainly didn't see all of their implications, but they gave Chloe some comfort.

'Papa…' Amy struggled in her arms, and Chloe leaned over, picking up Papa Bear and wiggling him in front of Amy. She quietened for a moment and then pushed him away.

'Okay then…' Chloe decided to try something different and started to hum the tune of the song that she'd heard Jon sing to her to quieten her tears.

It appeared that Amy liked rock 'n' roll a bit better. She settled into Chloe's arms, staring up at her face for a while and then reaching up, catching the dark yellow citrine that had slipped from the neck of her T-shirt and pulling it.

'No, sweetie, you'll break it.' Chloe pulled the chain

over her head, dangling the citrine in front of Amy, who batted it with her hand, seemingly mesmerised by its sparkle in the half-light.

'See how pretty it is? It's magic as well. If you hold it in your hand, it makes all the bad things in your heart go away.'

Chloe had needed something like that when she'd been ill. Something to help her summon her courage at the times she'd felt most alone. The crystal had been like a mascot, something for her to hold onto and remember the promises she'd made to herself.

And now she'd made a promise to Amy. She'd promised that, whatever happened, she would make things right, find a way to support Hannah so that she felt confident about being a good mother to Amy. That was one, inviolable promise that wouldn't be broken. Jon's promises to help might or might not be followed through, and Chloe couldn't bring herself to rely on them, however much the warmth in his eyes tempted her to.

'Mummy's coming back, sweetie. You'll see.' She whispered the words, cuddling Amy tight, and the child's eyelids began to droop.

CHAPTER SIX

HE'D SLEPT DEEPLY and for enough hours to make him feel human again. When the smell of cooking wafted up the stairs, Jon levered himself from his bed and made for the bathroom. But the time he'd emerged, the smell of coffee had been added to the mix.

He hadn't expected her to be cooking for him, and when Jon went downstairs to the kitchen-diner he didn't expect her bright smile either. Both were very welcome.

'What's that?' He craned over her shoulder as she slammed the lid down on a large electric waffle iron.

'Oat waffles. And coffee for you.' She switched off the coffee machine and put the flask of coffee on the table.

'You didn't need to do that.' He sat down anyway at the place that was laid for him. No one had cooked him breakfast since… Jon's mind recoiled at the thought. This was nothing like that, it was probably just a thank-you for taking care of Amy.

'A decent breakfast never did anyone any harm.'

That was obviously a matter of pride with her. Chloe's fridge was always well stocked with good, fresh food, and he didn't need to look in the larder to know that there would be fruit and vegetables there.

He poured the coffee, noticing that her cup stood next

to the kettle, with the tag from a herbal teabag hanging over the side. Chloe struggled momentarily with the waffle maker, and just as he was about to go and help her she got it open and the waffles out onto two plates.

'You like bananas?' She turned to him and Jon nodded. 'Good.'

A liberal helping of sliced banana, along with kiwi fruit and blueberries went on top of the waffles, and she carried the plates across. One waffle for her and three for him.

'You're sure you don't want any more?' Jon could eat three. He could probably eat half a dozen, but he didn't like the idea that she was giving him the lion's share.

'No, one's enough for me.' A glass jar with homemade nut butter clattered onto the table in front of him in a no-nonsense invitation to help himself. Then Chloe fetched her tea and sat down.

'These look really good.' Jon took a mouthful and it tasted even better than it looked. 'Where's Amy?'

'In her playpen, in the sitting room. Let's see whether we can get breakfast eaten before she realises we're not paying enough attention to her.'

Chloe managed it, and was halfway out of the front door before Amy started to grizzle. Jon's fuller plate was only part finished, and he picked it up and walked into the sitting room.

'It's just you and me, then, Amy. Let's see what we can get up to today.'

Despite all Chloe's misgivings, they'd fallen into a routine that worked. Every morning, she ignored Jon's assertions that he'd probably stumble across something that would pass for breakfast later and made a proper breakfast for all of them. And every morning he cleared his plate and said that he might be tempted into getting used to this.

Each evening was different, too. Someone to ask about her day, and give an account of how Amy had fed the ducks in the park, or almost managed to sneak a packet of chocolate buttons out of the supermarket without paying.

Amy was beginning to settle, and wasn't waking up so many times during the night. Jon and Amy had become firm friends. He talked to her all the time, and just the sound of his voice was enough to have her gazing wide-eyed into his face. Chloe sometimes envied her niece the privilege of looking at him so unashamedly when her own glances at Jon were so often stolen. The way Amy had no hesitation about being close to him, steadying herself against his legs as she heaved herself up into his lap, curling up there while he read the paper or a book.

But there was one, magic hour. After Amy was in bed, and when the house was quiet, they sat together in the kitchen, talking about everything and nothing. Jon spent two evenings assembling a moon and stars mobile to hang over Amy's cot that somehow failed to catch Amy's eye but which Chloe gazed at every night before she closed her eyes to go to sleep.

'She doesn't like my cookies, then?' Breakfast at six on a Saturday morning made jumbo sized cookies with elevenses all the more welcome. But Amy had licked the icing off hers and thrown the rest on the floor.

'Maybe she's just saving the world as we know it.' Jon took his second cookie from the plate, and Amy started to make loud explosive noises, clapping her hands together.

'Ah. And who taught her how to do that?'

'If you're going to make Dalek cookies, you can't expect them not to fight a bit before you eat them.' He bit off the Dalek's head, rolling his eyes at Amy, while the little girl crowed with glee. 'Although I've never seen a pink Dalek before.'

'The pink ones are the ones you have to look out for. Much more dangerous. And when I looked in the cupboard for some colouring for the icing, I only had pink.'

'That explains it.' He broke off a piece of his cookie, handing it to Amy, and she put it in her mouth and then spat it back out again. 'Actually, I don't think she does like them. I'll just have to finish them off myself.'

'I'll make some more. That's the last of them.'

He grinned, leaning back in his chair and reaching for the paper. 'I'll get blue food colouring when we go shopping.'

'Aren't you going to your house?' Chloe had expected to be alone with Amy today, but instead Jon had gone out for the paper and seemed ready for a lazy Saturday.

'The builders have it all in hand. But I suppose I should pop in later, just to see what they've been up to…' He paused for a moment and then put the paper down. 'I don't suppose you fancy coming with me? It's a mess at the moment, but I like to think it's got potential.'

'Bit like this place, then.' Chloe stared up at the sitting-room ceiling, wondering how many times she'd lain on the sofa, tracing the cracks with her gaze. Looking at the crystals on the mantelpiece instead had been an exercise in ignoring what she couldn't change and concentrating on something a bit prettier.

He chuckled. 'It's nothing like your place. Mine's *really* a mess. There's absolutely nothing wrong with this house that a bit of filler and a couple of cans of paint wouldn't remedy.'

Chloe quirked her lips downwards. 'That's what I reckoned when I moved in, over three years ago.'

'And instead you gave your sister a home and then battled a debilitating illness. I think you can be forgiven for overlooking a few cracks in the ceiling.'

And Jon knew how to forgive. He seemed to do it with everyone, apart perhaps from himself. 'Okay, then, I'll come. Maybe it'll give me a few ideas on what to do when I get a chance to get started here.'

Jon's house was the only one in a street of neat, sub-urban houses that looked ramshackle, the paint flak-ing off the downstairs window frames. The garden in the front looked as if it had been recently cleared, a few tree stumps sticking out of the sun-baked clay soil and an uneven pile of stones that must have once been crazy paving.

'Watch out. Don't step into any holes.' He grinned at her, taking Amy from her car seat and hoisting her up into his arms, where she couldn't get into any mischief.

Only the newly painted front door gave some clue that the house could be a lot more than it was now. Jon opened it, and when Chloe walked into the hall it was dark and dingy, no wallpaper, no carpets. But it had possibilities. The decorative newel post and the stair bannisters had been stripped down, and once a coat of paint was applied it would bring out the rippling shape of the turned wood.

'This is wonderful.' She turned, running her hand across the sitting-room door. It was caked with so many layers of paint that the mouldings had practically disap-peared, but it still had an original stained-glass panel, along with what looked like a decorative cast-iron back-plate for the door handle.

Jon chuckled. 'Not many people say that. But when it's all done, I think it'll look okay.'

It would look great. It all needed a bit of care and attention, and about a gallon of paint stripper, but Chloe could imagine the house, rising phoenix-like from the dust and the years of neglect. 'You have most of the original features still.' She looked up at the ceiling and saw moulded cornices and plasterwork.

'Yeah. The place belonged to an old guy who'd lived here all his life. He was a hoarder, and it was in a pretty bad state but relatively untouched. You couldn't get past the piles of newspaper to decorate.'

'But you saw something in it.'

'It looked like a challenge. As we cleared everything, we came across some lovely old features. And a few nightmares. All the kitchen floorboards had been soaked through and were rotten. It's a miracle someone didn't fall through them. And the wiring was completely shot—the electrician took one look at it and condemned it as unsafe.'

Despite his less-than-enthusiastic comments, Jon obviously loved this house. Who wouldn't? A chance to give an undiscovered gem a new lease of life.

'It'll be lovely when it's finished, though.'

He grinned. 'That's what I'm hoping. Careful through here, the floorboards have been taken up to run the cabling.'

Jon led the way through to the kitchen, which had obviously taken priority over the decoration of the hall-way. Almost finished, it was bright and gleaming, with honey-coloured wooden cabinets and black quartz-ef-

fect worktops, which sparkled subtly when the light
hit them.

Spotlights were sunk flush with the ceiling. Bright
chrome taps and a built-in hob and oven with chrome
trimmings. Grey slate on the floor. Chloe gasped.

'Jon… This is gorgeous.'

'Like it?'

'I'd kill for a kitchen like this.' The kitchen units ran
along two sides of the large room, and cardboard boxes
were stacked neatly along the third. 'What's going in
here?'

'I was going to carry the units and worktop on round,
but now I've seen it I'm thinking that that's more cupboards than I could possibly use. I quite like the idea
of having a table and chairs here instead, the way you
have in your kitchen. I think it would make the room
warmer.'

Chloe nodded. 'It is handy having the table, and the
room's plenty big enough. And it could do with a break
to all those clean lines.'

Jon chuckled. 'All I need is Dalek biscuits and a few
crystals. That'll take the gleam off it.'

'I'll send Amy round with the biscuits. You need to
get your own crystals.'

She walked to the back door, looking out on the
weeds and overgrown shrubs. Then they picked their
way past the lifted floorboards in the hall and up the
stairs to the front bedroom.

Another one of those breath-catching, I-wish-I-lived-
here moments. Jon had obviously decided to decorate
one room at a time, and this room had fresh paint on the
walls and woodwork. There was a cast-iron fireplace,
which had been stripped and polished up so that the
pattern of twisting stems and flowers shone. A curved

bay window, with stained glass in the lights at the top, looked out onto the quiet street. This would be a lovely place to wake up in the morning, dappled colour shining across the polished oak floor.

'I didn't notice these windows from the outside. They're the originals?'

'Yep. They were in pretty good condition under all the layers of paint. I'm not sure how warm they'll be in the winter, but I don't want to put in secondary glazing if I can help it.'

'Thick curtains? I have some with thermal linings in my bedroom and the room's really cosy in the winter.'

Chloe bit her tongue. She could almost see the kind of thing that would match the red and green in the stained glass and bring those colours out. A cold night, closed curtains and candlelight. And the warmth of Jon's arms.

But this wasn't her house. Amy would never sleep soundly in the next bedroom, surrounded by pretty things, and Chloe would never sleep in this one. Amy should be with her mother, and Jon had determinedly left all thoughts of a family behind.

Jon was nodding, looking at the windows. 'I didn't think of that. It's an idea.'

Amy started to struggle in his arms, wanting to explore, and Jon put her down onto her feet, holding both her hands and letting her lead him over to the fireplace. She traced the pattern in the cast iron with her fingers, sitting down suddenly in the hearth.

'So you have a kitchen and a bedroom…' It seemed like a countdown. How much more did he need to do here before he wouldn't need to stay at her place any more?

'And the bathroom's going in over the next few

weeks. That's all I really need, and then I can move in and do the rest as I go.'

'It's a long job.'

'I've found somewhere that I want to be now. If it takes a while to get everything finished, that's okay.' He looked around the room thoughtfully, and then bent to pick Amy up. 'I guess we should make a move if we're going to get some shopping.'

That was best. Get away from here before it gave Chloe any more ideas. She turned, almost bolting out of the room and down the stairs.

It had been right on the tip of his tongue. Jon had almost asked Chloe to come with him to choose curtains.

Calm down! he reasoned with himself as he walked down the stairs, his boots thudding on the bare wood. *Choosing curtains isn't like asking someone to kiss you.*

In some ways it was worse. A kiss could be explained away as the momentary wish for some warmth. Curtains were a more cool-headed statement. And the thought that Chloe might just talk him into the perfect set of curtains for the room was terrifying.

He was done with perfect. He didn't want domestic bliss because he'd seen it crumble into vitriolic chaos. Jon realised he'd left his car keys in the kitchen and left Chloe hovering by the front gate, walking the length of the hallway with Amy in his arms.

'Bye-bye.' Amy waved happily as he picked up his keys and closed the kitchen door behind him.

'That's right, sweetheart. Bye-bye, house. We're going to the supermarket now.'

Out of the mouth of babes… Amy's instinct had divined the truth before he'd had a chance to formulate it in his head. Helping a friend out was one thing. But he wasn't going to ask Chloe back here, for fear that he might be tempted to ask her to stay.

CHAPTER SEVEN

EVERYTHING HAD FALLEN into place. Jon's week off work was long enough to make sure that Amy had fully recovered, and Chloe had secured a place for her at the hospital crèche for the following week. Jon was working days now and their evening routine of cooking, eating, a bath and bedtime for Amy, followed by the precious 'magic hour', needed no adjustment. Hannah would be back home with James at the weekend, and Chloe was beginning to allow herself to believe that her return might be a step forward.

Jon had been too busy to take a break on Monday, but she'd bumped into him at the crèche on Tuesday, and they'd eaten their sandwiches together, playing with Amy. Chloe wondered whether he'd be there today, a little thrill of excitement pulsing through her fingers as she checked her phone.

Almost as if he knew she'd been thinking about him, Jon chose that moment to send a text.

Are you going to lunch now?

At some point they'd dispensed with the formalities of *Hello* and *What's happening?* Maybe because it felt that even though they were working at different ends of the hospital, they were still together.

Yes. Join me?

Busy with a patient. Do you have ten minutes? I'd like your opinion.

In A and E?

The thought was unexpectedly stirring. Jon's work in A and E was one area that was his alone and which Chloe didn't normally have any part of.

Yes. Won't keep you long.

I'll be right down.

She found him at the doctors' and nurses' station at the end of a row of cubicles, staring at one of the computer screens. He motioned for her to sit down in an empty chair next to him.

'Thanks for coming. I've got some X-rays I'd like your opinion about.' His brow was furrowed, and he was clearly wrestling with a knotty problem. Chloe resisted the impulse to wonder what she could possibly add to Jon's expertise, and hoped he wasn't over-estimating her experience.

'Okay.' She sat down, warily.

'What do you see?'

She looked at the X-ray on the screen in front of him. 'A pretty nasty dislocation of the big toe. Do you have the patient's notes?' She reached for the manila folder in front of him, and Jon put his hand on top of it.

'I just want to know what you see here. This is Patient A, right?'

'Okay. Well, Alan's got a dislocated toe.' She could hardly imagine that Jon hadn't seen that.

'Alan?' He shot her a suspicious look, as if she'd been looking at his notes behind his back.

'His name's on the X-ray, Jon.'

'Oh. Well, anyway, how might that have happened?'

'What is this? Have you asked Patient A?' Chloe rolled her eyes. Diagnosis wasn't a guessing game.

'Of course I have. I just want your professional opinion, without knowing any of the context, because, having seen both the boys, I'm struggling not to jump to conclusions.'

'There's a Patient B?'

'Yes. I'm coming to him.'

Chloe heaved a sigh. 'Okay, I'll play along. An injury like this is most probably caused by the foot coming into contact with something hard. Kicking a wall would do it, or a blow to the end of the toe. Something like that.'

'What about another child stamping on the foot?'

'It's possible, I suppose, but not likely. If that's what happened I'd be on the lookout for some underlying condition or deformity of the bones, which meant that a dislocation was particularly easy.' Chloe frowned at him. 'Jon, you know all this.'

He grinned. 'Yes, I do. I just wanted a second opinion.'

Chloe suppressed a smile. It was nice to think that Jon had chosen her for that. 'Have you relocated the toe?'

'Yes.' Jon punched one of the keys on the computer keyboard and another X-ray flashed up on the screen.

'It's been relocated and dressed. I'll be making an appointment for him up in Orthopaedics for ongoing care.'

Chloe studied the X-ray carefully. 'Nice job. I don't see anything here that concerns me. There's a tiny bone fragment there...' She pointed to the X-ray and Jon bent in to look.

'I didn't see that.'

The fragment was so small that it was almost invisible. But it was gratifying to be able to add even this to Jon's assessment. 'I'd say this is definitely an impact injury. Do you want to tell me what this is all about now?'

'In a minute.' He punched the keyboard again, and another set of X-rays appeared on the screen. 'Patient B.'

'Right.' Chloe scanned the X-rays carefully. Three different angles, showing the front and sides of a knee. 'Well, I don't see any fracture of the patella, although there may be a very small hairline one that won't show up on the X-rays until it starts to heal. There's another very small chip just here, and I'd like to have him back in a couple of weeks, just to check on that.'

'Caused by?'

'Impact on a hard surface most probably. I can't say any more that that, Jon. You're going to have to tell me what...' She glanced at the bottom of the screen. 'What Craig told you.'

'You've told me what I need to know.' He looked at his watch. 'Thanks. I won't take any more of your lunch break.'

'What? Come on, Jon, you can't stop there. What's happening?'

He grinned, as if he'd known all along that she couldn't confine herself to just answering his questions. 'Two boys, both twelve years old. They're in the school changing rooms so they both have bare feet and legs, and there are a lot of hard surfaces around.'

'Which would explain the dislocated toe.'

'Yes. Alan says that Craig stamped on his toe, and dislocated it. He jumped back and Craig stumbled, falling on the tiles.'

Chloe frowned. 'Well, I suppose that's possible. Not very likely though. What does Craig say?'

'He's not saying anything. Not a word. I've got a teacher from the school, and both mothers here, and all three of them want *me* to sort this out and tell them exactly what happened.'

'Well, you can't, not categorically. We can say what might have happened, but they're going to have to sort what actually *did* happen between themselves.' Jon knew that as well as she did. 'What's your interest in this?'

'I just want to know. Because if the cause of Alan's injury doesn't explain its severity, there may be some reason for taking a few more X-rays.'

True. But that was something that would usually be assessed in her own department, not A and E. Jon knew that as well as she did. 'And...?'

'Because we're not busy at the moment. And I'm on my lunch break.'

That wasn't good enough either. 'Yes. And?'

Jon puffed out a breath. 'Okay. If you must know, I think that Craig's been bullied. He has psoriasis, and Alan referred to him as "Flaky Craig" a couple of times when he thought that his mother wasn't listening. He's very obviously playing the victim with his mother and teacher, but he's quite cocky when they're not around.'

The look in Jon's eyes was reason enough. 'Would you like me to talk to him?'

Jon shook his head. 'I don't see...'

'Don't worry. I'm not going to confront him with anything.' This was perhaps one area where her experience was a little more useful than Jon's. 'I get the odd alternative version for how someone's come by an injury. A and E sometimes isn't the environment to tell your doctor that you broke your ankle having sex.'

'I don't know about that. We get our share of unlikely injuries. Goes with the job.' His brow creased. 'Someone broke their ankle having sex?'

'Don't ask. I still can't work out how she managed to get into that position... All I'm saying is that Alan might be a little more forthcoming with a different face. One that hasn't already been kind to him. You *have* been kind to him, haven't you?'

'Of course. It's not my place to judge anyone.'

'So why don't you let me give it a go? If his mother agrees.'

Jon got to his feet. 'Okay. I'll speak to her.'

Jon had spoken with Alan's mother and the teacher who was with the boys, and they'd agreed to sit out of his direct line of sight, while Chloe spoke to him. He wondered what she thought she might say that would convince Alan that the truth was better than the obvious lie he'd told.

Or perhaps she wouldn't need to say anything. She walked into the consulting room, leaving the door open so he could stand in the doorway with Alan's mother, watching and listening. Chloe was immaculate as usual, a dark skirt and shoes under a white coat. When she sat down opposite Alan, her smile was composed but held a touch of the confidante. Jon would have told her pretty much anything.

'Hello, Alan. My name's Dr Delancourt. I'm doing a survey—would you mind if I asked you some questions? About how you hurt yourself today.'

Nicely done. Alan nodded, and Chloe turned the page in the notebook she carried, taking a pen from her pocket.

'Thank you. It looks as if you've been in the wars.' Chloe flashed him a mischievous look. 'Did you win?'

Get the boy to brag a little. Jon felt Alan's mother shift uncertainly from one foot to the other beside him.

'Yeah, I won. I showed him.'

'I'll bet you did.' Chloe leaned forward a little, her elbows on her knees. 'So who did you show?'

'There's this boy at my school. When he takes his shirt off in the changing rooms his back's all flaky and horrible. I told him I didn't wanna see it and he needed to get out of there.'

Chloe nodded, as if that was perfectly understandable. Jon saw Alan's mother put her hand to her mouth, staring at the back of her son's head.

'And you had a fight with him?'

'He didn't wanna go. So I shouted it, right in his ear…' Alan stopped suddenly, perhaps realising that he was saying too much. 'That doctor. I told him.'

'Dr Lambert?' Chloe waved her hand dismissively. 'I don't like him very much. He's a bit starchy.'

Chloe's tone was so believable that Jon almost protested. It seemed that Alan agreed with her, though.

The boy leaned towards her, clearly about to impart a secret. 'I kicked him out. Flaky Boy.'

'Really?'

'Yes, really. I kicked his bottom and he ran away.'

'He must be very strong if that's how you hurt your

toe. I saw your X-rays, and it looked very painful.'
Chloe made the observation casually.

'It didn't hurt.' Alan's bravado belied the way he'd
howled when Jon had relocated his toe. 'And that Flaky
Boy's not strong. I kicked him and then he fell over onto
his knees. My toe bashed against the locker.'

'Oh, I see. Show me.'

Chloe was taking Alan through it all again so there
was no mistake, and tears were running down Alan's
mother's face.

'I didn't… We didn't bring him up to do this…' She
whispered the words so quietly that Jon had to strain
to hear them.

He nodded. 'It's okay. We just need to know, that's
all.'

Chloe seemed to have satisfied herself that Alan had
told the truth this time. 'Okay, Alan. I've got to go now.'

She stood and walked towards the door. Alan turned
his head, saw Jon and his mother and flushed bright red,
realising he'd been duped. 'I didn't do anything. That
bitch made me say it—'

'Alan!' His mother rallied suddenly. 'Don't you dare
use that word.' She turned to Chloe. 'I'm so sorry.'

'It's okay.' Chloe took her arm, guiding her away
from the doorway. 'I've been called worse.'

She glanced at Jon, then nodded in the direction of
the drinks machine. He caught her meaning and ad-
vanced towards Alan's mother. 'Why don't you come
with me? The nurse will keep an eye on Alan, and we'll
have a cup of tea.'

'What about Craig?' Alan's mother reddened suddenly. 'What am I going to say to his mother? If Alan's
hurt him…'

'Chloe, would you go and take a look at Craig?' Jon

imagined that her technique might be a little different with him, and that the boy would respond to her warmth and perhaps find the courage to voice what had happened to him.

'Yes, I'll go now.'

They'd managed to snatch ten minutes for a cup of tea together before it was time for Chloe to go back to work. Craig had told his side of the story to Chloe, as Jon had thought he might, and now the whole thing was out in the open and could be dealt with.

'Apparently it's not just Alan. Some of the other kids have been bullying Craig as well, but he was too scared to say anything.'

Jon nodded. 'Well, Alan's mother's determined to put a stop to it. That's a good start.'

'A very good start. Poor Craig. He had quite a bruise where Alan kicked him. And that knee's going to be painful for a while.'

'He'll go on your list for a follow-up?'

Chloe smiled. 'I've fitted him in. His mother's bringing him back on Friday and I'll take a look and see how his knee's doing once the ice has brought the swelling down a bit.'

Jon would have expected nothing less. 'Good. Thanks. And thanks for today, too. Remind me never to lie to you. I don't much fancy being on the other end of your interrogation techniques.'

'You were watching. I didn't do anything to Alan, just encouraged him to talk.' Chloe pointed her finger at his chest. 'You I'd be a bit rougher with.'

The temptation was a great deal more than he could be expected to bear. Jon leaned forward across the table.

'There's this new study, just come out. The moon's really made of green cheese, just as everyone thought.'

She snorted with laughter. 'I'll talk to you later. When we get home.'

It was another brick, cemented firmly into the wall. He and Chloe had joined forces to look after Amy, and it seemed that they were just as effective when they worked together. Her approach might be a little different from his, but their differences were what had borne fruit.

'I'll see you then.' He felt his pager buzz in his pocket, and gulped down the rest of his tea. 'Got to go…'

CHAPTER EIGHT

CHLOE SUSPECTED THAT there would be no talk of the moon and none of green cheese either tonight. When she'd picked Amy up from the crèche that evening she'd heard from one of the nurses from A and E, who had come to collect her son, that there had been a multiple car accident on the motorway.

Jon was late home, missing Amy's bathtime and the kiss goodnight. She was sitting in the kitchen, trying not to wait for him, when she heard his key in the door. The front door closed and she waited for him to appear. But there was just silence.

He was in the hallway, his hands in his pockets, his back leaning against the wall. Jon seemed wearier than she'd ever seen him. She walked up to him, touching the sleeve of his jacket, and he seemed almost surprised to find her there.

'Tough afternoon?'

He nodded. 'Yeah. I lost a patient.'

That was hard for any doctor. For one working in Paediatrics, there was an even keener edge to the blow. 'I heard there was an accident.'

He nodded, not meeting her gaze. 'A little boy. The paramedics had already revived him once in the ambulance, but he was failing fast by the time he got to the hospital. I couldn't do anything.'

'You tried, though.'

'Yeah. I tried.'

There was nothing she could say to him that he didn't already know. No way she could make this any better, because it was what it was. Along with all the young lives he saved, or made better, were the ones that Jon couldn't save. The day that didn't hurt was when any doctor should seriously think about changing their profession.

'Have you eaten? I'll make you something.'

'Thanks, but...' He shook his head. 'I'm just going upstairs.'

He obviously wanted some time alone. Chloe walked back into the kitchen and put the kettle on, more for something to do than because she wanted a drink. Sitting down at the table and ignoring the click as the kettle boiled and then switched off, she waited.

Ten minutes. From the creak in the floorboards, just outside her bedroom door, she knew exactly where Jon was. Perhaps he didn't want to be alone after all. Chloe walked upstairs, pausing at the open door of her bedroom. Sitting on the edge of the bed, one hand stretched so that his fingers were gently touching Amy's, Jon was watching the little girl sleep.

When he saw her he got to his feet, whispering so as not to disturb Amy, 'Sorry. The door was open...'

'That's okay. When I heard about the accident, I held her a little tighter.'

'We have to protect her.' Jon's face was anguished.

'We will.' Now wasn't the moment to point out that he didn't have to do anything at all, it was her job to protect Amy. For the moment, at least, he was a part of that. Chloe moved towards him, her trembling fingers reaching out to hug him, but he drew back.

Jon knew that a lot of his colleagues went home and hugged their kids after a day like this. But the way he'd wanted to see Amy, to check that she was still breathing, and that the world could continue to turn, had taken him by surprise.

He and Helen had made an agreement never to bring their work home. He'd stuck by that as best he could, keeping moments like this away from the quiet, gleaming perfection of their house. But as soon as Chloe had touched his arm, downstairs in the hallway, holding her had stopped being something he just wanted to do and had turned into something that he needed.

He'd settled for want, instead of need, and had gone upstairs to check on Amy. But now that Chloe was here… Jon reminded himself that she had her own issues about being touched, and that the intensity with which he wanted to touch her would probably be unwelcome.

But she touched him. He drew away and she touched him again, taking hold of the front of his shirt and pulling him towards her. And then she was in his arms. Chloe reached out, curling her fingers around his neck.

One breath. One look.

There was no longer any him or her, just one frozen moment in time, which they both owned equally. Chloe seemed to understand everything that was in his heart, every question and every sadness. He buried his face in her hair, hanging onto her as tightly as he could.

He was holding her so tight against his chest that she could hardly breathe. Or maybe it was just that her heart was beating so fast that her lungs couldn't keep up.

'I'm sorry…' She felt his arms loosen around her.

'No… Jon, don't be sorry. You shouldn't be sorry for anything.' She didn't want him to push her away now. It was too soon, and the connection that pulsed between them too strong.

She felt him sigh as he gently wrapped his arms around her again. It wasn't quite as thrilling as being crushed against his body, but it was close.

He held her for a long time, neither needing to say anything. But they couldn't stay like this for ever, even if that didn't seem like such an outrageous idea at the moment.

'Tomorrow's another day, Jon.'

He nodded, letting go of her. The room seemed suddenly freezing cold as he gave Amy one last look and then walked out into the hallway. 'I thought I might—'

'Go for a run?' She smiled at him. Chloe was getting to know Jon's coping strategies. He was often up early, running for the joy of it, before she and Amy had gone downstairs to start their day. In the evenings it was different, something to get the cares of the day out of his system.

'Yeah.' He narrowed his eyes. 'You haven't taken up mind-reading, have you? Those crystals of yours…'

The crystals had become a joke between them. When she'd been ill, it had helped her calm her mind to focus on their sparkling depths, in the same way that running cleared Jon's mind.

'Don't knock it. Each to their own.'

'Whatever gets you through the night, eh?' He grinned and suddenly he was very close. He brushed a kiss on her cheek, and almost before Chloe could feel the scrape of newly grown stubble on his chin he was gone, walking into his own room to change into his running gear. In half an hour he'd be back again, out of breath from pushing himself to the limit on the last mile, that easygoing smile returned to his lips. And everything would be back to what passed for normal these days.

This was hopefully the last time they'd have to do this, because James would be bringing Hannah home the day after tomorrow. Amy was bathed and in her pyjamas and Chloe sat down on the sofa, with Amy next to her, positioning her laptop in front of them.

'Mummy…' As usual the sound of the video conferencing call tone prompted the word. In a little less than two weeks Amy had learned to associate the shrill tone with her mother, as if Hannah were now locked away inside the computer. Chloe tried not to think about it too much, because it was heart-breaking.

James answered, looking tanned and smiling. He turned from the screen, beckoning to someone, and Hannah came to sit next to him.

'Mummy!'

'I love you, Amy.' Hannah blew kisses to her daughter, and Amy wriggled forward towards the edge of the sofa, trying to get closer.

Hannah was smiling, but it seemed as if it was an effort. Her eyes had dark circles under them, and James had his arm protectively across the back of her chair, as if he was ready to give her a hug if needed.

'Say, "Love you, Mummy."' Chloe leaned over towards Amy, whispering in her ear. Amy turned to her, her small hand on her cheek.

'Love you, Mummy.' Amy repeated the words perfectly, but she was looking in the wrong direction. Straight up at Chloe.

'No, sweetie...' Chloe swallowed down her embar-
rassment, trying not to look at Hannah, and then jumped
as the front door slammed. Jon had been working late
but he was home now. Amy looked round and, forgetting that her mother was on the screen, started to crawl
to the far end of the sofa towards the open door of the
sitting room.

'Hello, Amy...' Jon popped his head around the door
to greet her, and then saw the laptop on the table. 'Oh.
Sorry to interrupt.'

'That's all right. Come and say hello.'

If all three of them were in one place, on the sofa,
and she held Amy facing the screen, then there could
be no more mistakes. Maybe Jon caught the look of
desperation that Chloe gave him because he walked
straight over and sat down, retrieving Amy and putting her on Chloe's lap.

'Hi, Hannah. How are things?' Jon leaned in a little
so that Hannah and James could see him.

'I'm okay.' Chloe looked up at the screen and into
Hannah's face. There was no sign that she'd heard what
Amy had said, and maybe the words had been lost
somewhere between her laptop and James's.

'We went sailing yesterday,' James broke in.

'Yeah, and you nearly went over the side.' Hannah
smiled suddenly, nudging her brother, and Jon laughed.

'I would have liked to have seen that.'

'No, you wouldn't. If I was going to get wet, then I'd
have made sure you did too,' James retorted, and Chloe
began to breathe again. She hugged Amy, directing her
attention towards the screen, as James and Jon traded a
few good-natured insults, and Hannah joined in, saying a bit about what they'd been doing on their holiday.

'So what are the arrangements for Saturday?' Fi-

nally James got around to the one day that everyone
was thinking about and not mentioning.

'I thought I might drive up with Amy tomorrow night
and stay at your place, if that's okay. Then we'll be there
when you get back, the following morning.'

James nodded. 'Yeah, that's fine. Sounds good.'

Hannah was biting her lip. 'There's no rush.'

Chloe swallowed down her disappointment. It
seemed that Hannah had mixed feelings about coming
home. 'I'm really looking forward to seeing you. And
Amy's been missing you, of course.'

'I miss her too.' A tear rolled down Hannah's cheek,
and James put his arm around her. 'But she's... She
looks so happy. And you love her, don't you...?'

'Yes, I love her. So do you.' Chloe felt as if she were
walking a tightrope, and there was a very long fall beneath her. Telling Hannah that she'd loved having Amy
here might imply that this was a state of affairs that
could continue. Telling her that she had to take Amy
back now might put her under too much pressure.

'But you and Jon... You can both look after her so
much better.'

Jon leaned forward towards the screen, speaking
gently. 'Hannah, there *is* no me and Chloe. I'm moving out in a few days' time.'

Good. That was right. Hannah seemed to be taking
it for granted that the very temporary family that had
been created here could last. Maybe *she* was at fault for
giving that impression. Maybe Hannah had seen her
body language and had realised how much she'd fallen
into depending on him.

'I just think...' Hannah shook her head, as if what
she thought didn't matter.

'Hannah, there's no pressure for us to do anything

right now. I'm taking the next two weeks off work so we can spend some time together. I'll be right there to support you and Amy in any way I can.'

Hannah nodded, wiping her eyes. 'Yes. Okay.'

This was always the way with Hannah. The less she said, the more overwhelmed she was feeling. It was probably best to let things rest for now.

'So I'll see you all on Saturday.'

'Yes.' James answered for Hannah. 'That'll be great.'

They'd talked for a while longer, and even though James and Chloe were both obviously concerned, they'd stayed positive and smiling for Hannah's sake. Amy was becoming drowsy, but Chloe managed to get her to wave and blow kisses to her mother before they ended the call.

Chloe leaned forward, closing her laptop, as Amy snuggled against her. At a loss for anything to say that might help, Jon went into the kitchen and made her a cup of tea.

'I hope I said the right thing. About my not being around for much longer.' He put her tea down on the coffee table in front of her.

'It was exactly the right thing.' Chloe turned her worried face up towards him. 'All of this is about Hannah wanting the best for Amy. Right now, she's feeling so worthless and scared that she thinks that I can give Amy more than she can. But I can't.'

Jon sat down on the sofa next to Chloe, and took Amy from her so she could drink her tea. The little girl stirred and then went back to sleep. No doubt the moment she was taken upstairs and put into her cot, she'd be wide awake again.

'Have you considered the possibility that it might be

better to keep Amy with you for just a little while longer?' Jon chose his words carefully.

'I'll look after Amy for as long as it takes. But Hannah will never get over it if she gives Amy up, and neither will Amy. I've just got to give Hannah the right support.'

'You and James, you mean.' Jon couldn't help smiling. Chloe was so determined to do this alone, and it was oddly gratifying that her unwillingness to take any help extended to James as well as him.

'Me and James, then. Obviously. Although he has his own family to think of, and he doesn't have as much time as I do.'

They sat in silence for a moment, and Chloe sipped her tea. Despite all the uncertainties, all the loose ends, this seemed somehow right. The three of them against the world.

'Hannah never said anything to me about Amy's father.'

Chloe shook her head. 'He's not on the scene. Very deliberately so. We know who he is, he went to the same school as Hannah. It seems that he and Hannah had something going together, and when he went off to university they split up. When Hannah ran away, that's where James found her. Living with him in his student halls.'

'Didn't anyone notice?'

'Apparently not. He used to smuggle her in at night and back out again in the morning. Hannah spent most of the day in coffee bars. When we realised she was pregnant, James went to see the family, but the boy said it was nothing to do with him and his parents didn't want to know either.'

'That must have been hard on Hannah. Has the boy

ever been in touch?' It would be hard on Amy too, when she was old enough to understand. Jon held the sleeping child a little closer.

'Not once. Hannah decided not to pursue it and I couldn't help agreeing with her. If someone lets you down that badly, you're better off without them.'

'I suppose so. Still hurts, though.'

'Yes, it does still hurt.'

Chloe's face showed no emotion, but Jon suspected that she was talking a little about herself, as well as Hannah. Someone had let her down, and she'd decided that she should deal with everything on her own, now.

'You know I didn't tell the exact truth when I said I'd be gone in a couple of days, that was really just for Hannah's benefit. You're off for the next two weeks, and I've given the hospital the time I promised them. I have the next three weeks off.'

'That's supposed to be for you to finish the renovations on your house. So that you'll have it all done when you start work permanently. You agreed that with them.'

'I told you I'd be around to help, and I will be. The builders are putting the new bathroom in, and I can put anything else off until later.'

He could see the disbelief in her eyes, and all he wanted to do was to show her somehow that he really did mean what he said this time.

'Yes, I know. Thanks.'

Chloe's words offered him little comfort. Because, whatever she said, he knew that she didn't believe him.

CHAPTER NINE

JON MADE SURE that he was home from work early the following evening so he could see Amy and Chloe off. It had just been two weeks but now that he was putting Amy's things into Chloe's car, and about to kiss the little girl goodbye, it seemed impossible that he could have come to care so much about her in so short a time.

'I'll be back on Sunday evening.' Jon thought he saw Chloe's lip tremble.

'Yeah. Give me a call if that changes. You never know, I might cook you dinner.' Jon was banking on having the weekend here alone, and he didn't want Chloe walking in on him unannounced.

'It's not going to change. I've said I'll go in to work on Monday for a few hours to do a handover. But you don't need to cook. I'll have had Sunday lunch with the family.'

Jon congratulated himself silently on clearing the final hurdle before his plan could be put into action. 'Okay. Well… Good luck. You'll give me a call if there are any problems, won't you?'

'Yes, I will. Thanks.'

They stood facing each other in the hall. There was nothing more to say, and they both had things to do, but something kept them both glued to the carpet. Finally Jon put his arms around her shoulders.

The awkwardness of it was melted away by the scent of her hair. Chloe clung to him, and he felt himself let out a breath. This was crazy. It was just a weekend.

'Go...' It seemed altogether wrong to let her go anywhere, now that she was so close, but somehow he managed to take a step back.

Chloe looked up at him and the now-familiar feeling of honey oozing across his senses almost made his knees buckle. Then she reached up, standing on her toes to plant a kiss on his cheek. She drew back, almost before he had a chance to register it, walking into the sitting room to fetch Amy.

'Say bye-bye.' Chloe waved her hand, and Amy followed suit. 'See you again soon.'

Amy repeated the words almost perfectly, and Jon gave her a hug and a kiss. Then he walked them out to the car, standing to watch as they drove away, feeling suddenly as if the bottom had just dropped out of his world.

His cheek still burned where her lips had touched it. But now that Chloe had gone, he had forty-eight hours to put into operation the plan that he'd been fine-tuning for the last week. The challenge got him moving, and he strode into the house to fetch his jacket and car keys.

Everything he needed was piled up in the hallway of his house. A thank-you to Chloe for coming to his rescue and letting him stay here for the last month. Something that was easy for him to do and not so easy for her to achieve. And he hoped she'd love it.

Chloe drew up in the road outside her house, sitting for a moment in the car to gather her thoughts. She'd almost managed to believe that everything was going to be all right, that Hannah would find the confidence to take the first vital steps in taking Amy back to look after her. But everything had fallen apart.

The aching tiredness made her feel almost physically sick with instinctive fear. Chloe reminded herself that this was nothing like what she'd felt when she'd been ill, and that there was a good reason for it. Getting out of the car, leaving her bag still on the back seat, she pulled herself straight and walked to the front door.

Another instinct, this one more recently formed, made her wonder whether Jon would be there. He'd said that he would, and Jon hadn't broken a promise yet, but everything else had gone horribly wrong this weekend. Why not this?

When she opened the front door, the smell hit her and for a moment she was too fatigued to even know what it was. As she twisted the handle of the kitchen door, she realised. Paint.

Maybe Jon had brought something home to paint at the kitchen table. When all she really wanted was a cup of tea…

He *was* sitting at the kitchen table, the look on his face something like that of an agonised boy who had hoped to do something right. Chloe looked around. The kitchen looked suddenly lighter and she couldn't understand why for a moment.

It was the new paint on the ceiling and walls. The unusual tidiness of her worktop was because the old one had been cleared and removed and a new one installed. She realised that it was the same worktop she'd admired at Jon's house, and the new doors on the kitchen cabinets were the same honeyed wood. Her old cooker had been cleaned to within an inch of its life and a couple of new spotlights, placed unobtrusively in the darker corners, made the room seem about twice the size.

She took a step inside, her legs almost failing to hold her. Beneath her feet, the old lino had been taken up and the quarry tiles underneath gleamed.

For a moment she couldn't speak. Chloe walked over to the window and saw that the frame had been sanded down and painted—a proper job, not just a lick of paint to cover whatever flaws were hidden beneath it. It hit her suddenly that this was Jon's thank-you to her. He hadn't needed to give her a leaving present, certainly not something like this, but that was what it was.

And she'd given him everything he needed to work with. Chloe realised that the jokey conversation about colours and styles, what she'd do with the kitchen when she had the time, had all been noted down in his head. She'd even lifted a corner of the lino and shown him the quarry tiles underneath, saying she'd hire something to polish them up one day.

'You…' Jon's voice was uncharacteristically full of doubt. 'You could say something…'

No, she couldn't. This was all too much. She'd lost almost everything this weekend, and now she was losing Jon. Chloe felt herself choke, and a sudden burst of energy took her up the stairs to fling herself onto her bed to sob into her pillow.

Jon ran his hand across the wooden tabletop, which just thirty-six hours earlier had been in the garden, being sanded and polished. Maybe everything she'd said last week, about how the colour scheme he had in his kitchen was the one she wanted in hers, had been just idle talk, and not what she wanted at all. But she'd seemed so sure, as if she'd thought about it, and no one could deny that the kitchen looked great.

Or maybe she'd wanted to do it herself. That was a possibility, but Jon knew that she didn't have the time or the energy at the moment. Maybe she was just overcome with delight… Jon shook his head, burying it in his hands. Unless Chloe's delight looked a lot like dismay, that wasn't very likely.

He hadn't heard from her over the weekend and he'd assumed that things were going the way she'd hoped. But that could just be wishful thinking on his part. Would she really have given him a call to tell him that there was a problem?

Something was wrong. His decision to stay here, because Chloe obviously wanted to be alone, was dropped and Jon walked slowly up the stairs.

He tapped gently on her bedroom door and received no answer, so he pressed his ear against it. He couldn't hear Chloe moving around, so he knocked again, this time a little louder.

She'd heard him. A rasping breath that sounded as if it was laced with tears came from the other side of the door.

'Chloe… What's wrong?' he called to her, and there was still no answer. He supposed he could just go downstairs and leave her with whatever it was that was bothering her, but the thought that his actions might have been the cause of her tears glued him to the spot.

He could wait here, or go in. Waiting was obviously about as much good as going back downstairs, so he twisted the door handle slowly, ready to apologise and bang the door closed in his own face if she was undressing. But she wasn't. He knew she wasn't.

Just in case, he called her name again and told her

he was coming in. There was still no answer, and he opened the door. Chloe was sitting on the bed, her face buried in her hands.

'Chloe... I'm sorry. I really thought you'd like what I did...' Suddenly it all seemed like a very bad idea. Why hadn't he left well alone? Or just bought her a bunch of flowers.

'It's lovely...' She gulped the words through her tears.

So that wasn't what she was crying about. Or if it was, they were the oddest tears of joy he'd ever seen. He walked towards her, bending down to disentangle the strap of her handbag, which was still over her shoulder, and laying the bag on the bed.

'Chloe...? What's the matter?' She hadn't told him to go yet, and if that wasn't exactly an invitation to stay, he wasn't too proud to take it as such.

She seemed to be making an effort to pull herself together, and Jon pulled a tissue from the box next to the bed and handed it to her. Chloe blew her nose and he handed her another for her eyes.

'Thank you for the kitchen. It looks fantastic.' She heaved a sigh. 'You really shouldn't have done it.'

'Well, I wouldn't have if I'd known it was going to drive you to this.' He'd been telling himself for the whole of the last week that this was just a thank-you. That it was something one friend could do for another. But now he realised that all he'd really wanted to do was make her smile. Give her something that she loved.

He wanted to hug her and dry her tears, but he made do with sitting cautiously down on the bed next to her. 'What's the matter, Chloe?'

She shook her head, reaching for another tissue to

finish mopping up the tears. 'I'm sorry. It's been a difficult weekend.'

'Want to talk about it?'

She shook her head but didn't move. 'I've put too much on you these last two weeks. And now you've done this…' She turned her honey-brown gaze on him. Now, more than ever, it reminded him of sweet pleasure, dripping over his senses.

'I'm here to listen, Chloe.'

'I know you are. But it doesn't matter…' She gave him a teary smile. 'I'll make some supper. We have to have something nice to christen that gorgeous kitchen with.'

She stood up, obviously bent on going downstairs and pretending that everything was all right. He couldn't bear it. Jon caught her hand, pulling her back down onto his lap.

'Forget the kitchen.' It had been the centre of all his hopes and efforts for the last two days, but now he didn't care about it. 'I'm not letting you go until you tell me.'

He had hardly touched her, and the force that had impelled her into his arms must have come from somewhere inside herself. And although he was hardly holding her at all, she couldn't escape. Maybe because her own fingers were clasped tightly together behind his neck.

He must have spent the whole weekend here, working on her kitchen, when he should have been at his place, working there. Of course he'd wanted her to be delighted with it. It was a wonderful present, and she didn't know how she could ever repay him for it.

One thing she was sure of. Tears were no kind of thanks and sharing what had happened this weekend wasn't either. Because he'd only feel that he had to stay, when what he should really do was go and get on with the things he had to do.

But she so wanted this. His strength and solidity. The feeling that she could face anything if he just held her for a little while.

'The kitchen's beautiful. It's a lovely goodbye present.'

He raised his eyebrows. 'It was more of a thank you than a goodbye. Why, are you throwing me out?'

'No.' She nudged her head against his shoulder. 'I'm telling you that you've done enough. You don't need to hang around here, sorting out my problems.'

'So I can stay as long as I want?'

'Of course you can.'

'Where's Amy? Is she back with Hannah now?'

'No, she's with James and Carol.'

'And Hannah?' Chloe didn't answer and his arms tightened around her, pulling her closer. 'You said I could stay as long as I wanted. I'm taking that as an invitation to pry into your personal business as well. I'm not letting you go until you tell me.'

Chloe sighed. There was no way out of this. She was going to have to tell him and *then* perhaps he'd leave Hannah to her.

'James dropped Hannah off at her place on his way home. She said she wanted to do some things there, and that she'd come round after lunch. We waited until three o'clock, and when she didn't answer her phone, we went round there. Hannah had gone.'

'Gone? Where?'

'I don't know. She left a note saying she needed some more time and that it was better for Amy if she was with us right now.'

'And you haven't heard from her?'

'I texted her, and she replied. She says she's okay but she won't say where she is. She promised to text this morning, and she did.'

'So you left Amy with James and Carol'

'I left her there because I'm going to look for Hannah.' The resolution that had taken hold of her, and strengthened over the last twenty-four hours suddenly hardened into certainty. 'I'm going to find her.'

'Do you know where to even start?'

'I'll call her friends. Maybe I can persuade Hannah to tell me where she is, or to come back here if she's not ready to go home. I don't know. Something's got to work.'

Chloe fell silent for a moment, letting herself feel his body against hers. It was a small indulgence, which would have to last through all of the uncertainty of the days ahead. Then she pulled away from him and stood up.

'We should make waffles.'

He looked up at her. 'Waffles? You're sure about that?'

She shrugged. 'James and I have looked everywhere locally we can think of. There's nothing more I can do tonight. I just have to trust that Hannah's being sensible and that she's all right. And I've got some bananas in the car.'

He grinned. 'Banana waffles. Sounds like a plan.'

She made a show of opening and closing all the new cupboard doors because she could see that it pleased him. 'How did you do all this in a weekend?'

'I got into the swing of it when I did my own kitchen. And it's really just cosmetic. The cupboards were good, and they're a standard size, so I just put new doors on them.'

Chloe ran her hand across the worktops. 'They're lovely. They must have cost a fortune. You must let me '

He laid one finger across her lips, grinning. 'No, you don't. My builder gets a trade discount on everything. And the length of worktop that I didn't use in my own kitchen turned out to be almost enough.'

'So you're trying to kid me that you got all this for free? I don't believe it.'

'Believe whatever you like.' He grinned at her. 'Is it what you wanted?'

'It's better than that. It's gorgeous, and I can't believe you did it all in two days.'

'I had a bit of help, fitting the worktop.'

'Your builder again? The one who gets everything free?'

'Yeah. He's a great guy.'

Chloe wondered whether she should press the point. Jon had obviously spent something on this, but he was unwilling to tell her how much and she should probably accept the gift gracefully. And the most valuable part of it was the thought and care that had gone into it. He'd listened to what she wanted and had made it all happen.

'It's wonderful. I can't thank you enough.'

He grinned. 'It's my pleasure. Now, get on and make the waffles. I'm getting hungry just thinking about them.'

They ate together, taking their time. By the time they'd done the washing up, exhaustion started to kick in for the second time, this time leaving Chloe with little choice but to recognise it.

'You look tired.' He seemed to be reading her mind.

Or more likely he'd noticed that she could hardly keep her eyes open.

'Yes. Think I'll have an early night.'

'What time are you going into the hospital tomorrow?'

'Uh?' Chloe could hardly think, let alone plan. 'Not early. About ten, probably…'

'Okay. I'll see you in the morning, then.'

CHAPTER TEN

EVEN THOUGH SHE'D been tired, she hadn't slept well, and when Chloe woke early she knew that she had no chance of dozing off to sleep again. Dragging herself out of bed, she stumbled to the bathroom and stood for a long time under the shower.

When she went downstairs, Jon was in the kitchen. His face took on a pained expression when she sat down at the table.

'Did you sleep at all?'

'Not much.' Chloe twisted her mouth downwards, pushing her hair back behind her ears. 'Just tell me I look better than I feel and make some coffee, eh?'

'Right you are. You look gorgeous, by the way.'

'Thank you.' She sank her head into her hands 'Don't overdo it, I might think you're not being sincere.'

He chuckled and made the coffee. Then he fetched her a bowl of muesli and watched her eat it.

'Are we ready to go, then?' He put the empty bowl in the sink.

'We? Are we going somewhere?' Jon's breeziness was obviously concealing some kind of plan.

'I'm popping up to the hospital. I need to get some forms from the HR department. I'll run you in and then we can go and get some lunch, if you like. Think about your next move.'

'Are you sure?' The HR department sounded a bit like an excuse, but Chloe was too tired to argue.

'Yes. Come on. We'll stop and get some more coffee on the way.'

The second cup of coffee had finally woken her up, and by the time they arrived at the hospital Chloe was feeling ready to face the day. She spent two hours handing over to the colleagues who were filling in for her, and found Jon waiting for her in the reception area, talking to an elderly lady with her arm in a sling.

He got to his feet when he saw Chloe. ''Bye, Mavis. Hope they sort your arm out.'

'I expect they will, dear. Don't forget what I told you.'

'No, I'll keep it in mind.' Jon took Chloe's arm and hurried her through the double doors of the department.

'What are you not forgetting?'

Jon shrugged. 'That turnips are high in calcium. Mavis has osteoporosis so she's dispensing advice to the whole of the waiting room about how to keep your bones healthy.'

'Good woman. But, then, you already know how to keep your bones healthy, you're a doctor. Which gives you no excuse not to eat your turnips.'

'Yeah. I thought I'd skip that piece of information, in case she expected me to comment on her X-rays. Fancy a pizza for lunch? We could leave the car here and walk down to that place in the High Street.'

Despite all of the worry that she must feel for Hannah, Chloe still managed to smile, and Jon couldn't help but respect her for it. They talked over lunch, and there was no trace of resentment for all that Hannah had put her through. Just determination to find her sister and somehow make things right again.

'Do you know many of Hannah's friends?' As they walked out into the afternoon sunshine, turning into one of the backstreets that led back to the hospital, Jon's thoughts turned to the next task.

'Quite a few of them. She has some down in Cornwall, from when she lived there with Aunt Sylvie. A few in London. James and I made a list, and I'm going to work through it this afternoon.'

'What if Hannah hears that you've been phoning round, looking for her? Won't she take exception to that?'

'I sent her a text this morning. I thought it was best to be honest and tell her what I'm doing, and that it's because I love her.'

'I think you're right—' Jon broke off as Chloe stumbled suddenly, his arm shooting out instinctively to grab her around the waist and stop her from falling. 'You okay?'

'Yes… Yes, I'm all right.'

She didn't look all right. She was so pale that she would have made a good addition to any Halloween party. 'Sit down for a moment.'

He looked around, and in the absence of anything more suitable Jon guided her to the low front wall that divided someone's front garden from the street and sat her down on it. If anyone objected, he'd tell them he was a doctor.

She was rubbing her leg, just above the ankle. Jon couldn't see any abrasions or swelling.

'Have you hurt yourself? Let me take a look.' He

knelt down in front of her, reaching out for her ankle, and she moved it away. 'Chloe…?'

'It's all right. I'm okay, just… I expect I tripped on that paving stone.' She nodded towards an uneven bit of pavement just where they'd been walking when she'd fallen.

'I expect you did.' Suddenly he realised. She was *hoping* she'd tripped, instead of her legs just giving way beneath her. 'How much sleep did you get over the weekend?'

'Not much.' She looked at him miserably.

'And you didn't sleep last night either. And you've been under stress for the last couple of weeks.' He asked the question that he didn't want to ask, and Chloe obviously didn't want to answer. 'Any tingling in your legs? Or pain?'

'I…don't think so.' She seemed suddenly unable to make her mind up. 'They feel a bit achy.'

'Your legs do ache when you're overtired.' He reached forward, taking her hand in his. 'Chloe, look at me. Now take a breath.'

The first try was more of a shiver than a breath, but the second was a little better. He nodded her on and the third was a good attempt.

'That's good. Now, you know as well as I do that a complete relapse for Guillain-Barré is so rare that we can discount it. Don't you?' He wanted her to say it, but she just nodded. That would have to do.

'Right. And you also know that some of the symptoms might recur from time to time, but that they'll be minor and we can deal with them.'

This time she said it. 'Yes.'

'Now we've got that out of the way, I want you to tell me truthfully whether you have any pain or tingling in your legs. Or if there's any reason for you to believe that you just didn't trip over that paving stone.'

'My legs ache, that's all. I...don't know.'

'Okay, well, that's good. Because being afraid is okay. I would be if I'd been as ill as you have. But I think you'd know if this really was Guillain-Barré and not just the stress you've been under, both physically and mentally.'

'Yes. I think I would.'

'So do you feel all right to stand now? We'll take it slowly back to the hospital.'

'Yes.' She seemed to suddenly pull herself together, smiling up at him. 'I'm okay.'

'Good. Take my arm.'

'I can walk...' She got carefully to her feet, ignoring his outstretched hand.

Jon grinned at her. 'I know. Just humour me, will you?'

She smiled, the warmth in her eyes trickling over his senses. Every time. He was like a bee, unable to ignore the honey in her smile.

He wouldn't let her fall. Not now, and not in the uncertain days that lay ahead. Jon was sure of that now, and all he had to do was to persuade Chloe to let him stay beside her.

When they got home, he made her sit down in the living room and put her through an examination that was rather more for show than anything else. The touch of his fingers as he slipped off her sandals. The look in his eyes as he carefully massaged her feet, his gaze searching for any reaction in her face.

There was a reaction all right. Probably not quite the one that he'd been aiming for. The warm glow of knowing that she was safe in his hands had been tempered by the spice of arousal.

'I'm diagnosing you as stressed and worn out...' He sat down next to her on the sofa, his arm resting on the cushions behind her head. 'And I'm prescribing some sleep. Do you think you can manage that?'

'Yes, but...' What she really wanted—really *needed*—was for Jon to hug her. Just to hold her and tell her everything was going to be all right, because if he said it she knew she'd believe it.

'But what?' He traced his finger around her jaw, tipping her chin up so that he could look into her face. When she reached out for him he was there, wrapping his arms around her and holding her tight.

'I'm sorry. I know I'm being silly...'

'Stop right there. I don't want to hear anything about you being silly or not being allowed to feel anything.'

'But—'

He drew back a little and put one finger over her lips. 'Not a word. You've been stronger than anyone should be expected to be. If you didn't stumble a little from time to time, I'd be tempted to diagnose you as not human.'

Maybe he was right. Maybe the years of making herself cope alone *had* stripped her of a little of her humanity.

'And what would you prescribe for that?' He was so close, and before she could stop herself Chloe stretched up, brushing a kiss against the side of his mouth.

Jon smiled, slowly. 'That would be a treatment option.' He kissed her back, but so fleetingly that she'd hardly tasted him before he drew away again.

'So you're starting with a low-level approach? Or is

that just the best you can do?' She grinned at him to let him know that she knew full well it wasn't.

'No. But we both have our limits.'

Yes, they did. His was that he couldn't believe that even the perfect relationship could work for him. Hers was that she couldn't bring herself to rely on anyone.

'I don't think I've reached mine yet.'

'Neither have I…' He kissed her again, and this time she could feel it. Sweet electricity, flowing through her and making her toes tingle.

His hand moved up her back to her neck. She could feel his fingers in her hair, his thumb brushing the sensitive spot behind her ear, and Chloe shivered.

Jon's mouth curved into a smile, just a breath away from hers. His thumb increased its pressure, making a small circle around the point that was driving her crazy.

'Not fair…' She whispered the words against his lips.

'I found it.' There was a possessive note to his voice, as if now that he'd discovered what he could do with that square inch of skin, he owned it. Maybe he was right. Chloe let out a gasp, tipping her head back, and he brushed a kiss against her neck.

It was a sweet foretaste of what sex might be like. The thought that he might seek out each one of the sensitive points on her body, before concentrating on the more obvious erogenous zones, almost made her cry out. It might take him a long time to find them all…

She took his head between her hands, kissing him on the mouth. That was what turned *him* on, she could feel it. When she just took whatever she wanted. He was strong enough to find that erotic.

And strong enough to stop when it seemed as if there

was no stopping either of them. Ending the kiss, hugging her tight against his chest.

'It would be nice…' Chloe buried her face in his chest so he couldn't see her disappointment. It was impossible for this to go any further and that had been clear right from the start.

'It *was* nice. But maybe we should leave it at that. And maybe you should try to get some sleep.'

She'd had a glimpse of the Jon who was capable of taking everything, but now his arms were gentle again. And suddenly Chloe felt that she could lay her fears aside and sleep.

'I'm very tired…'

'Good. Lie down, then.' He let her go and Chloe curled up on the sofa. 'I'll go and get something to cover you up.'

'But if Hannah calls…' She'd kept her phone with her night and day, ever since Hannah had gone missing, and even now it was sitting on the coffee table in case it rang. Chloe reached for it, hugging it to her chest, wondering if she'd wake if her sister called.

'I'll take it. Just sleep now.' Chloe felt him prise the phone from her fingers and she closed her eyes, drifting off to sleep.

When she woke she was warm under the quilt that she usually kept folded at the end of her bed and the curtains were closed, sunlight filtering through the cracks on each side of the window. She stretched, rubbing her eyes to focus on the clock on the mantelpiece, and saw a note on the coffee table beside her. Not bothering to get up and open the curtains, she reached for it.

I took your phone.

Yes, she remembered that. She wondered where he'd taken it.

My builder called and I've gone to my place for half an hour. If you wake up before I get back I strongly suggest you go back to sleep immediately.

The loop of the 'J' at the bottom of the note curled around in what might be a kiss or might just be a flourish. Chloe's fingers flew to her lips as they started to burn with the memory of his.

She sat up, smoothing her crumpled T-shirt. Maybe she could forget all about the kiss and just pretend it hadn't happened. She imagined that Jon probably wanted to. A shower and a change of clothes seemed like a good start to make.

She was walking back down the stairs when the front door opened. Jon was back, and suddenly she was wide awake.

'How are you feeling?'

'Much better, thanks.' Seeing him again made her body react immediately and her cheeks started to burn.

He was either pretending not to notice how embarrassed she was or he was blind. 'You've only just woken up?'

'About fifteen minutes ago. Jon…' She was trembling, hanging onto the bannister, hardly trusting herself to walk down the remaining stairs towards him. His gaze met hers, and in the warmth of his gentle blue eyes it was suddenly possible to say the words.

'We're okay, aren't we?'

He smiled. 'I'd very much like us to be.'

'Me too.' Suddenly everything moved into sharp

focus. She didn't want to lose the friendship they had. Not for the dream of something they couldn't have.

She walked downstairs, slipping past him and into the sitting room, opening the curtains and folding the quilt that had covered her. When he appeared at the door, she gave him a bright smile.

'Everything all right at your house?'

'Fine. They just wanted to make sure they had lights positioned right in the bathroom and along the hall. Hannah called.'

Chloe caught her breath, dropping the quilt onto the sofa. 'While I was asleep?'

'Yes, I was on my way back here. I managed to pull over in time to answer it.'

'What did she say?' She searched Jon's face for some clue as to whether this was good news or bad, but there was nothing. It was probably just news, because one call wasn't going to solve everything.

'She told me that I should make you stop looking for her. I asked her how she thought I was going to be able to make you do anything you didn't want to, and she loosened up a bit.'

'Thanks.' Chloe imagined that Jon's warm, easygoing tone was the best way to approach Hannah at the moment. He'd probably done a lot better than she could have.

'I told her that you loved her, and that the two of you should talk. That you had no expectations and you were willing to listen to whatever she said.'

'Thank you. That's good.' Very good. Chloe *was* willing to listen but she might not have thought to say it. A thought struck her. 'So how did you leave it? Is she calling back?'

'No. I'm not having you staring at the phone, waiting for her to call. I told her you'd call her.'

Chloe wouldn't have dared be so assertive with Hannah. 'When?'

'Half past five. That gives you half an hour…' Chloe grabbed her phone from his hand and he caught her wrist before she could call.

'No, Chloe. Not like that. Take your time, get your thoughts together and call her in half an hour. You need to do this on your own terms, as well as Hannah's.'

He was right. There was no point in working herself up into a panic and then saying the wrong thing to Hannah. 'Are you strongly suggesting that's what I do?'

A slow, lazy smile spread across his face. 'Yeah. Right in one.'

CHAPTER ELEVEN

SOMEHOW, IN JON'S COMPANY, the dreaded phone call didn't seem so bad. When the time came to make it, she felt almost relaxed, sitting on the sofa next to him.

'I'll wait in the kitchen.' Jon got to his feet.

'Would you stay? I'd...like you to stay, please.' The words still sounded odd in her mouth. But she wanted Jon to stay with her, the way he'd been right at her side through all of this.

He sat back down again. 'You'll have to tell Hannah that I'm here.'

She nodded and looked at her watch. Still two minutes to go but she couldn't wait. Chloe found Hannah in her contacts list and dialled, putting the phone on loudspeaker.

Hannah answered on the second ring.

'Chloe?'

'Yes... Hannah, I'm so glad to hear your voice. Jon's here with me.'

'Yeah? So I suppose I can't ask what's going on with you and him, then...'

Chloe swallowed hard, feeling herself redden. Even if it had just been her and Hannah, she wouldn't have known the answer to that.

'You can ask.' Jon's voice was good-humoured.

'Only if I asked you what was going on in your love life, you'd tell me to mind my own business...'

'Me? I'm about as single as it gets. It's you two I want to know about.'

Chloe wondered whether Jon had been quick-witted enough to turn the question around and find out whether Hannah was with someone. But he was giving nothing away, smiling into the phone as he replied.

'Nothing going on here either. But Chloe needs to know whether you're okay.'

'I'm fine. Good, actually. And there's no point in looking for me because I haven't gone to stay with any of my friends.'

Chloe felt tears prick at the corners of her eyes and pressed her lips together. Jon had been keeping the conversation light, and that was the way it should stay.

'Hannah, what do you expect her to do? If Chloe went missing, you'd look for her, wouldn't you?'

'She wouldn't...' Hannah's voice was tinged with disbelief, but the silence told Chloe that she was thinking about it.

She plucked up the courage to ask the one question that had been hammering in her brain constantly for the last two days. 'Why did you go, Hannah?'

There was a pause at the other end of the line. 'Look, I'm sorry about that. I heard James and Carol talking. James said some things...'

Chloe's mouth went dry. James could be outspoken at times, and Chloe had no doubt that he would have told Carol what was on his mind. 'James says a lot of things, you know that. But he does love you.'

'I know. And what he said he was right.'

'Right?' Something cold twisted around Chloe's heart. This didn't sound good. 'What did he say?'

'He said that if I was going to just leave Amy with you every time things got difficult, she'd be better off without me.'

'Well, that's wrong and James needs to apologise for saying it. You've always taken care of Amy.'

'You don't know, Chloe. I can barely hang on myself some days, let alone take care of Amy. James is right, she would be better off with someone else. Someone who'd love her the way that you do.'

'Me?' Chloe's mouth went dry. How many times over the last two weeks had she wished that Amy was her child, and that she could look after her for ever? This must be some kind of punishment for wanting things that she had no right to.

'You do love her, don't you?'

'What I want is for Amy to be with you. You're her mother…' Chloe looked around wildly, trying to think of something that would persuade Hannah.

Jon was there. Again. Always. 'I don't think this is a conversation that you can have on the phone. You need to talk face to face. What do you say, Hannah?'

There was a long silence, before Hannah replied quietly, 'Okay.'

'Good. Chloe, what do you think?'

In the warmth of his gaze she could suddenly think clearly again. It was time to draw some boundaries. Hannah had to know that she was loved, but she also had to know that her actions had consequences.

'I think… What do you say we make a deal? I know you need some time to think but I need to see you.' Chloe took a deep breath. 'Next Saturday.'

That was five days away and it seemed like an age. But if Hannah would agree to sit down and talk then Chloe could agree to wait.

'It's a long way...'

'I don't care if you're camped out on the moon. Where are you?'

'Remember when I was fifteen. We were going to go on a trip together but we never did get to go.'

Chloe's hand flew to her mouth. 'I'm so sorry...'

'That doesn't matter. I know you meant to take me, but you were ill. But I finally made it back, Chloe...'

'That sounds great, Hannah.' Chloe almost choked on the words. 'You can show me around.'

'Yeah, I'd like that. Saturday?'

'I'll be there. Saturday.'

'I'll be there too. I've got to go now.'

Hannah sounded as if she was crying, but that was okay, because Chloe was crying too.

'Will you call me? Or when can I call you?'

'I'll call. Every evening at eight, I promise. I do have to go...'

'I know. That's okay. I love you, Hannah.'

'Love you too.'

The line suddenly went dead. Chloe stared at the phone for a moment, trying to take in the enormity of what had just happened.

'Where is she?' Jon's quiet voice broke the silence.

'She's in the village where my father was born and where my parents met. In France.'

Chloe seemed almost in shock. That was understandable after the conversation she'd just had. But she'd stood up for herself, let Hannah know what she needed, and Hannah had responded to that. A trickle of pride ran through his chest, making him shiver.

He picked up the phone, putting it out of Chloe's

reach on the mantelpiece. The crystals could look after it for a few minutes.

'What did Hannah mean? When she said she'd finally made it?' He decided to start with the least emotive question he could think of.

'My father never talked much about his family or the place he was brought up. We went back to France every year on holiday, but never there. I suppose that James and I were less curious, because we had more time with our parents, but Hannah was very young when they died. My father's village took on a special significance for her. I think she thought that somehow she might find them there.'

'And you were going to take her back?'

'Yes, I told her I would. I was saving up so we could go there together, but then I became ill and we never did get around to going.'

'Perhaps it's herself she's looking for. As well as your parents.'

'Maybe so.' She heaved a sigh. 'I guess…well, perhaps that's something we can share. And perhaps I'll find some way of convincing her.'

'I imagine she's thinking pretty much the same at the moment. That she's got to find some way of convincing you.'

She quirked her lips downwards, then stood up and stretched her limbs, as if they ached from being in one position for too long. 'Whose side are you on?'

Hers. He was on Chloe's side, and always would be, irrespective of whether she was right or wrong. 'I'm… not really on anyone's side.'

'But?'

Yes, there was a *but*. One that had been bothering Jon

for a little while now. 'I think that Hannah's doing this because she's trying to force you and James to listen…'

'I know.' Tears welled in Chloe's eyes and Jon made himself look away before he gave in to the temptation to hug her and wipe them away. He'd gone too far once today, and a second time wasn't going to help. 'I know, I should have listened to her more…'

'That's not what I'm saying. You've got one solution to all this in your head and Hannah has another. You're trying to persuade her and she's trying to persuade you, and it's not going to work. You need to go right back to the beginning, and tell her how you feel about things, get her to tell you what she's feeling.'

Chloe was trembling, wiping the tears away. 'I want to listen to how she's feeling. I'm trying…'

'Have you told her how you feel? That you feel you've let her down?'

'No, of course not.' She turned suddenly, walking to the mantelpiece and picking up her phone. As if all of her fears, all her worries were centred around it. Then she put it back down again.

'Maybe you're right.' She twisted her mouth in an expression of regret and then the determined smile broke through. If he hadn't been trying so hard not to touch her, Jon would have seriously considered kissing her. 'So… What do I do next?'

It wasn't just a matter of what Chloe did next. In a moment when all he'd wanted to do was make her know that she was far stronger than she gave herself credit for, he had kissed her. And ever since that moment he'd been afraid to touch her again, knowing for sure now that her intoxicating sweetness had the power to overcome his better judgement.

What *he* had to do next was make a decision. Because the only way that they could regain the easy friendship, which had blossomed as they'd looked after Amy together, was to move past the kiss.

'What do you say to getting something to eat and then going for a walk? Somewhere nice. We have the time, and we can forget about all of this for a few hours and take a deep breath.'

She nodded. 'Yes. I'd like that.'

They'd decided against the local park and had taken a drive instead. Jon parked his car at the foot of the hill at Alexandra Palace, and they'd toiled up the steep incline. The breeze was still warm and the lights of London began to emerge through the gloom as dusk fell.

They picked out landmarks on the horizon, laughingly correcting each other when they got them wrong. It was nice. Companionable, as if they were learning to be together again, without flinching away each time they almost touched. Chloe took his arm in the darkness, giving silent thanks that she hadn't lost him.

As they walked back down to the car, she felt that she could breathe again. Start to plan. And it seemed natural to share those plans with Jon as he drove them home.

'I can sort out my plane tickets tomorrow. Fly down on Friday to meet Hannah on Saturday.' The little details, the ones that she knew she could accomplish, were the ones that she should tackle first.

'You could. Or we could drive down together. Take two or three days, find somewhere off the beaten track to stay.'

'That's…' There was no reason why not. Apart from the feeling that dashing down there somehow fitted the urgency of the situation. 'I should be… I might be needed. Somewhere.'

'You might. In which case you won't be around and everyone's just going to have to cope. I'm sure they'll manage.' He shot her a smile, his face angular, a different kind of handsome in the moving shadows.

'It doesn't seem right. James and Carol are looking after Amy and—'

'They'll cope. They have three kids of their own, and Amy will be fine. It strikes me that, however things turn out, this is going to be a long haul. You've got to pace yourself, give yourself a breather from time to time.'

That was good advice. Maybe she should use what time she had and take things a little slower. But maybe not with Jon.

He parked the car in the street outside her house and she got out, stretching her cramped limbs. Home. The last few hours had seemed as if she'd taken a holiday, and it felt as if there should be shoulder-high weeds growing in the front garden, but it was just the way she'd left it.

'I should go on my own. It's good of you to offer, but you have things to do here.' She followed him up the path, searching for her keys in her bag.

'Nothing that won't wait. I'm pretty sure that my house will still be there when I get back.'

'That's my point. It'll still be there, and still need to be done when you get back.' She walked through to the kitchen, putting her keys on the table. 'You don't have a magic kitchen that transforms itself when you're not there, like I do.'

He chuckled quietly. 'You still like it?'

'No. I still *love* it.' She turned to face him in the shadows. 'This is the dramatic pause before I put the light on and see it all over again.'

Actually, the dramatic pause wasn't so bad in itself. She could get lost in that and forget all about the kitchen, staring up at that easygoing smile, which seemed tempered by steel in the shadows.

'Why don't you trust me?' Suddenly he seemed a little more steel than smiles. 'You trust this.'

He gently pulled the gold chain around her neck, freeing the citrine from under her sweater. Chloe realised that her hand had automatically gone to her chest to feel its shape.

'This was given to me by a friend when I was first ill. It was on a silver chain and it broke, but I loved the colour of the citrine and I put it on another chain. The chain was my mother's.'

'So you kept it by you?'

'Yes. When I was alone it…helped me cope.'

'So these crystals *do* have magical properties.' The look on Jon's face said that he didn't believe that for a second.

'I'm a scientist, like you. I believe in what I can quantify. Would you say that the human mind has no bearing on the body?'

He chuckled. 'I've worked in A and E for far too long to think that.'

'Or that holding onto good memories can't get you through the bad times?' She curled her fingers around the citrine.

'No, I wouldn't say that either.' The corners of his mouth turned down. 'But it's not easy to take second place to a piece of crystal, hung around your neck.'

'You're never second best.' Her answer came a little too quickly, too fluently to be anything other than the absolute truth. 'I just don't want to take advantage of you.'

'So you push me away?' He looped his arms loosely

around her. 'Don't do it, Chloe. I know you've been let down before but I'm not going to repeat history.'

'How would you know that?' She suddenly wanted so badly for him to be different, but couldn't dare to believe he was.

'Because I've made up my mind.'

She felt her fingers curl, bunching his shirt in her hand. 'We all make our minds up about a lot of things.'

'Okay. So someone promised they'd be there and then wasn't. Your parents?'

'No. I know they would have been there if they could. Hannah was the one who felt deserted when they died, not me and James.' She moved away from him, and he let her go. Chloe almost wished he'd put up more of a fight and crush her against him, the way he had before. But that had got them nowhere and had only threatened their friendship.

'I had a boyfriend.'

'Ah. A nice boyfriend?' There was a touch of the competitiveness she'd heard in his voice when he'd been talking about the crystal. Jon really didn't like to be second best.

'Fair to middling. We'd been going out for a couple of years and I really liked him at the time. When I was sick he held my hand...not that I could feel it, mind you, because my right hand was paralysed, but I suppose the thought was the main thing.'

'I imagine so.'

'Anyway, he promised me that he was going to be there for me, through thick and thin, whatever happened. That we were going to do this together. I was so grateful to him, and I loved him more than anyone at that moment.' Chloe could feel tears pricking behind her eyelids, and blinked them away.

'Just that moment?' There was only tenderness in his voice now.

'Well, a bit longer than that. A week or so. When I got to rehab he only visited once a week, and by the time I got home he'd gone.' Chloe gulped in a breath, trying not to feel the awful loneliness she'd felt, stuck at home, unable to do anything but wait and hope. 'I heard that he'd been crying on my best friend's shoulder and telling her he couldn't cope.'

'*He* couldn't cope?'

'Well, apparently she couldn't either. Neither of them came to tell me, but when I asked around I was told they were going out together. They had me in common, you see. Both of them were pretty upset about what had happened...' Chloe couldn't keep the bitterness from her voice. And that wasn't fair.

'I don't blame them. It was a lot to ask, it was obvious that I was going to need a lot of help over a long time. But they might have had the decency to come and tell me, you know?'

'That's the least they could have done.' He caught her hand, clasping it to his chest.

'You feel that?'

'Yes, I do.' His heart was beating under her fingertips, strong and steady. The kind of heart you'd want on your side whenever times were tough.

'I promise that I might be there for you, as a friend. I might not, depending on the circumstances.'

She couldn't help laughing. It was honest, at least. 'That's good. Thank you.'

'And I promise that if I tell you I'm going to do something, I'll do it. No excuses, no half-measures.'

'That's very good.'

'And I'm telling you that I'll come to France with you

and stick around for a while. Not for ever. I have to go back to work in three weeks, and if the builders manage to knock my house down I might have to pop back and survey the wreckage. But I'll be there for as long as I can, and I'll do whatever I can to help.'

'That's perfect. I'd like that very much.'

'So that's settled, then.' He smiled down at her. 'Now, are we going to switch the light on and see whether any of the handles have fallen off the kitchen cabinets while we've not been looking?'

CHAPTER TWELVE

IT WAS A strange feeling, inhabiting the space between what was possible and what he wanted. But they'd drawn the lines carefully, and they both understood the boundaries. Those boundaries allowed them the freedom that the kiss had threatened to take away. That casual give and take, which meant they could just enjoy each other's company, without having to examine every touch, every word for a meaning that shouldn't be there.

And luck seemed to be on their side. Tickets and hotel reservations were obtained without too much trouble, and Hannah kept her promise to call the following evening. On Thursday they were up early and ready to go, in the bright crispness of a late summer's morning.

'You're sure about this?' Jon gave her one last chance to go inside and change her clothes.

'Positive. A hundred miles south of here, it's going to be much warmer.' She had a fleece jacket on over a summer dress. He could almost smell the yellow and blue flowers sprinkled across the light fabric.

'All right. Whatever you say.' The morning was imbued with a kind of excitement that was more akin to a new adventure, not the urgency of an emergency where every second counted. For the next two days he had

Chloe all to himself, and as long as they covered the miles, they could do whatever else they liked.

With one, significant exception. Now that he had nothing else to do but keep his eye on the road, Jon had to remind himself that the boundaries they'd set were all for the best, and that *whatever they liked* didn't include stopping the car and claiming Chloe's lips again.

He hadn't been able to keep up with her rapid French when she'd booked their accommodation, but Jon assumed she'd booked a couple of motorway hotels, and doubted they'd provide the ambience for anything other than a meal and some sleep. Which was just as well because, however much he wanted to kiss her—however tantalising the thought of exploring a little further than just a kiss—that was one avenue that should remain closed to them.

By the time they emerged from the Channel Tunnel the sky was looking a lot more promising, a dark clear blue that seemed to beckon them towards the horizon. Sixty miles of motorway driving and then Chloe suddenly indicated a left turn.

The next twenty miles got them no closer to their destination as she turned the map one way and then another, trying to puzzle out where they were going. Somehow they managed to get back on track and Chloe directed him through a set of large, wrought-iron gates and along a long avenue, edged with trees and dappled by sunlight.

'Wow. Look at that.' The avenue had opened up into a wide, sweeping curve, which grazed the entrance of a magnificent chateau. White painted and gleaming in the afternoon sun, it looked like a fairy-tale castle, complete with turrets at each side.

'This is it.' Chloe pointed to a cluster of cars to one side of the entrance. 'I think we can stop there.'

'We're staying *here*?' Jon had imagined that they might be just passing, to find some more modest accommodation somewhere in the grounds.

'Yes.' She turned to him, her face shining. 'Do you like it?'

'I love it, but…' It hadn't been quite what Jon had had in mind when he'd said they'd find somewhere to stay.

'It's my treat.' Chloe shot him a warning glance as he opened his mouth to protest that she hadn't needed to do this. 'Don't argue. You've done so much for me, and this is just to show you how much I appreciate it. I hope the inside is as nice as the outside.'

That would be difficult. The chateau stood in rolling countryside, dominating the landscape. It looked as if the one and only cloud in the sky had landed here, depositing this elegant, fairy-tale castle just to give ordinary mortals a blueprint for the proportions that they should build in.

But somehow the inside was even better. A soaring hallway that managed to be both grand and welcoming, its relaxed elegance extending to the other rooms they passed as their hostess led them up a sweeping staircase and along a wide corridor.

Right at the end, the woman opened a door, speaking in French to Chloe. 'She says she hopes we don't mind a climb.' Chloe responded in French, shaking her head and smiling.

The stone steps wound around a stairwell. Above him, Jon could see layer after layer, like the swirling, ever smaller spirals of an ancient sea creature. Here, the elegance of the rest of the building had been left behind in favour of white-painted stonework, which seemed older and much more utilitarian.

They were both out of breath by the time their hostess unlocked a door that led off the stairs a couple of turns before they got to the top. She beckoned them inside and Jon caught his breath.

The room was enormous, the square back giving way to a huge curve, which must follow the shape of one of the turrets he'd seen from the outside. High windows gave a spectacular view of the countryside, and on this side of the room a stone fireplace, big enough to roast an ox in, was stacked with logs. The bed was big enough to overpower almost any room, but here it looked almost insignificant, standing to the side of the curved space.

'This is amazing. I feel as if I'm in a castle...' Jon dropped their bags, wondering whether Chloe had booked just the one room. That thought sounded even better than their surroundings.

But their hostess beckoned to them again, leading them up to the top of the spiral staircase outside. 'This is your room.' Chloe grinned at him.

It was much the same as the room below, with an even more spectacular edge. In the centre of the curved space a domed glass ceiling let sunlight flood downwards, right onto the bed that was placed beneath it. Jon imagined that its occupant would be able to see the stars at night.

'This is...' He shrugged, smiling. 'Words fail me.'

Their hostess laughed, dropping the keys into Chloe's hand. An exchange in French and she left them alone.

'It's better than the pictures.' Chloe was smiling broadly. 'Our very own castle for the night. You said it would be good to get away for a couple of days.'

'I'm not sure I was imagining we'd do it in this style.'

He walked to one of the windows, looking out. 'If any of our troubles try to get at us we'll be able to pour boiling oil on their heads as they scale the walls.'

'Or you can plunge a sword through them as they make a rush for the stairs.' Her laugh sounded as if she really had left the world behind, and that nothing could assail her here. 'Madame says that we can get up to the roof from here.'

An alcove by the door gave way on one side to a shining bathroom, the large bath standing right in the middle of the room. On the other side, another set of winding stone steps led up to a door that opened onto a flat roof, the glass dome sitting at the centre of it but leaving more than enough space around the edge for a table and chairs, sheltered by the high stone ramparts.

'We can have dinner up here if we like. Although the dining room looked lovely in the pictures.'

'Here. Definitely here.' They only had one night to enjoy this and they should make the most of it. Chloe had made him a make-believe king of a fairy-tale castle, and she was his queen. Her hair was loose at her back, her dress moulding her legs in the breeze. Her honey-brown eyes were bright with excitement. All he really wanted to do at this point was kiss her.

Maybe that would happen. It seemed as if almost anything could happen here, but for now he was content to stand with her, looking out across the gardens at the back and the sweep of the drive at the front. The road seemed a very long way away at the moment, toy cars buzzing back and forth along it. Tomorrow his would be one of them, but that seemed such a long way away that it wasn't even worth considering.

CHAPTER THIRTEEN

THE CHATEAU HAD exceeded her expectations. But best of all was Jon's reaction. She could see that he loved it, and more than that he seemed to have left behind the urgency of the road, and that was exactly what she'd wanted. He needed a break as much as she did, if only he'd admit it.

They still had the rest of the afternoon, and they'd decided to walk down to the village together. Three kilometres of sunshine and birdsong. The scent of flowers in the hedgerows and the quiet buzz of insects. He took her hand, winding his fingers loosely around hers, and everything in the world seemed right.

Sitting on a bench in the village square, watching the world go by, was the only thing on their to-do list. Until Jon suggested hot chocolate, which posed a whole new set of important questions. They took their time answering them, inspecting each of the three cafés set around the square and finally decided which was best.

'It's a long walk back to the chateau.' His smile was delicious, warm and relaxed. 'Do you think we should force ourselves to have a pastry as well?'

More decisions. Chloe had already been eyeing up the choice on offer, and didn't know which to pick. She pushed the menu card across the table towards him.

'You choose. Something that's rich and sweet and really, really bad for us.'

He grinned, beckoning towards the waitress. 'I see you're coming around to my way of thinking…'

It was a succession of one delight after another. They'd indulged in hot chocolate and wickedly delicious pastries, then walked back to the chateau together. They explored the downstairs rooms and then sat on the terrace at the back for a while. Chloe had asked for dinner on the roof, and they'd chosen what they wanted from the menu, then gone back to their rooms to change.

She chose a summer dress with a matching lace woollen shawl, glad to find that they hadn't creased too much in her bag. A little make-up seemed only right, and she brushed her hair carefully, catching it back in a loose arrangement at the back of her neck. As a compromise between wanting to look her best and wanting it to seem that she hadn't spent too much time on her appearance, it would do.

When she ventured up the spiral staircase she saw that the door to Jon's room was open. He turned from the window, his face breaking into a smile.

'You look beautiful.'

A lump lodged in the back of her throat. He was wearing a simple dark blue shirt, open at the neck, with dark blue trousers. Jon looked even more effortlessly gorgeous than usual, slim-hipped and broad-shouldered, the strong set of his jaw giving a delicious sense of purpose to the softness of his eyes.

'Thank you.' Telling him that he looked beautiful might be misconstrued. But he did.

'What do we do to let them know we're ready for dinner? Or do we just wait and see what happens next?'

'Oh. No, we phone. I have the number.' Chloe pulled her phone from the pocket of her dress and dialled.

He helped her up the steps to the roof. Perhaps he knew that her knees were shaking. The evening was warm enough to leave her shawl on the back of the chair, and when the waitress arrived with their meals and lit the candles on the table, the shelter of the stone ramparts stopped them from blowing out immediately. She wished them a smiling *'Bon appétit!'* and left them alone, flipping a switch at the top of the stairs, which lit a string of fairy lights that ran all the way around the edge of the tower's roof.

It was a shame, really. Jon had ordered a very good wine, and the meal was well worthy of more attention than Chloe could give it. But the spectacular view and the fairy lights, which seemed brighter and more magical as the sun went down, were also entrancing. And Jon...every move he made, every gesture and every smile made her forget about everything apart from him.

'Would you like a dessert?' They'd taken their time over the meal, talking as darkness fell.

'Just coffee for me.' It was a little cooler now, and Chloe wrapped her shawl around her shoulders.

'I think even I can manage that.' He grinned, reaching for her phone and asking for two coffees in halting French.

The waitress appeared again, bringing coffee and clearing the table, leaving their glasses and the bottle of wine behind. Chloe sipped her coffee and then reached for the bottle. Jon hadn't refilled her glass while they ate, and it was still more than half-full.

'Not yet.' He laid his fingers on the back of her hand. 'I want you stone cold sober.'

'What for?'

He smiled. 'A turn around the roof? Don't want you falling over the edge.'

That was hardly likely. She'd have to ask him for a leg up if she was going to climb across the wide stones that protected them. All the same, Chloe left the wine where it was and stood up, taking his arm.

Two steps, three… They got almost halfway round before he kissed her, and when he did she was almost trembling with anticipation. The breeze tugged at her senses, making her shiver as he drew her into the warmth of his body.

She wrapped her arms around his neck, staring up into his eyes. 'I didn't mean…for this to happen…'

'You don't want it to?' His hands were spread possessively across her back, and he made a show of moving them so she could step away if she wanted to. He didn't need to, the kiss had told them both exactly what they wanted.

'No, I…' Chloe thought hard. Now wasn't the time to be at all unclear about what she wanted. 'I love that it's happened. I just didn't plan for it…'

'Ah. So you didn't lure me here to have your way with me? I'm afraid that I didn't lure you either.'

'You didn't? I think the least you can do is pretend you planned it all.' She stretched up, brushing her lips against his mouth.

'You'd be very disappointed in me.' He leaned towards her, whispering in her ear, 'I don't have any condoms but that doesn't mean we can't just…improvise a little.'

His fingers moved on her back and Chloe shivered at the thought. She'd take a bet that Jon improvised very, very well. But he didn't need to.

'Actually, you know that I packed a travel kit to give

to Hannah? Things she might need, that she probably didn't think to take with her when she left.'

He chuckled quietly. 'You thought she'd need condoms?'

'Well, you never know. I thought it wouldn't hurt to cover all the possibilities, particularly after last time…' She didn't want to talk about that now. She wanted to kiss him again.

'You are the most resourceful woman.' Clearly he liked that because his kiss almost lifted her off her feet. 'What next, now that we can do whatever we want? I have no expectations…'

She was stone cold sober and she knew exactly what she wanted. 'I don't have any expectations of you either. Can we take the rest of that bottle of wine downstairs with us now, and find out what happens next?'

'That sounds wonderful.'

He kissed her again and she felt his body hard against hers. One hand on her back pulled her in tight against him, the other caressed her jaw, sending shivers of sensation through her. His fingers brushed the sensitive spot right behind her ear, as if he'd remembered how it turned her on, but he wasn't getting to that quite yet.

Instead, she felt his hand move, trailing across the neckline of her dress and lower to cup her breast. At last. It felt like fire, out of control and spreading through the whole of her body.

He responded to her whimper of pleasure by backing her against the high stone ramparts. Her gaze locked with his, as he rubbed his thumb gently over the material that covered her nipple, and when she caught her breath he smiled.

'You feel so good. I want you so much.' He whispered the words into her ear.

That was just fine with her, as long as he took it slowly. The sudden urge to be taken right now, right here had receded into a hotter, more unrelenting fire and she wanted this to last.

'Not yet. Not for a while…'

'You want to drive me crazy?' Jon's gaze burned its way into her senses.

'Yeah, that's the plan. You want to come downstairs?'

Before he let her go, there were more caresses, leaving her in no doubt that Jon intended to show her exactly who was boss, and for her to tell him so. Which was fine, because when she moved her hips against his, his gasp held all the surrender that her whispered words had.

He held the moment for as long as it lasted, his eyes dark in the moonlight. Then he turned, taking her hand and leading her downstairs, picking up her phone and the bottle of wine on the way.

'Not here…' Chloe took her phone from his hand, calling downstairs to say that the waitress could come and clear the coffee things now and that they wouldn't be wanting anything else. Then she led him downstairs to her room, locking the door behind them.

Jon reached for the box of matches on the high mantelpiece and bent to light the candles that stood in the grate. Soft light danced through the room.

Standing between the fireplace and the four-poster bed, he kissed her again, while she struggled with the buttons on his shirt. When she'd pulled it off, he slowly undid the first of the row of buttons that ran down the front of her dress.

One more, and then another. Jon was obviously

enjoying the suspense as much as she was, and she watched as he deftly undid each one.

'You're better with buttons than I am.' She smiled up at him as he slipped her dress from her shoulders and it fell to the floor.

'I've got a good reason to be. You're very beautiful.' The way he was looking at her made her feel beautiful. Made her feel strong.

He ran his finger along the chain that encircled her neck, and when he got to the citrine, nestled between her breasts, he was suddenly still. 'I'll take care of you tonight, Chloe.'

She believed him. The citrine had been all she'd had once, but Jon was here now. 'Will you take it off for me?'

He turned her round, sweeping her hair to one side. She felt him open the catch and then he put the citrine and its chain into her hand.

'Look at me…' Turning her round again to face him, he tipped her chin up. His face held all the promise of pleasure. 'How does it feel when I touch you?'

'It feels wonderful.' She knew what he wanted her to do. He wanted her to put the citrine aside and rely on him completely. That was what she wanted too, but suddenly in the back of her mind the memory formed, clear and insistent, taking her back to a time when every touch had been potentially painful, every loss of control had had to be fought. She felt her hand instinctively close around the citrine.

The moment of uncertainty must have shown in her face and she felt his fingers curl around hers. 'Chloe, you can hold onto this if you want. It doesn't matter.'

She could see that it did matter to him. And it mattered to her, too.

'You'll be there for me? This is the first time…since I've been ill.' She knew that shouldn't matter, but the softness in Jon's eyes told her that he understood.

'I'll be there with you all the way. I promise.'

She reached behind her, putting the citrine and the chain down on the cabinet beside the bed. When Jon kissed her, she didn't miss it at all.

He finished undressing her, caressing her as he did so. Watching for each response until cause merged into effect and all she could feel was one delicious impulse of pleasure and wanting. She reached for the waistband of his trousers, unfastening it.

'I want to touch *you*, now.'

Jon had known that Chloe might hesitate. Known that he must be gentle and watch for any sign of uncertainty on her part. But he hadn't dreamed that she would speak so openly about how she felt, or that it would change their lovemaking so profoundly.

Because speaking about it had seemed to break every barrier. Every touch was met with a word or a sigh. She didn't leave him to guess what she was feeling, she told him, and that empowered him.

When she touched him, it was like electricity running across his skin. Her finger, her tongue tracked delicate patterns of delight across his body, as slowly they pushed each other further.

'Chloe… Chloe…' If he'd known what to beg for he would have done it. His whole body was shaking, sweat trickling down his spine and adrenaline pumping through his veins. And when he touched her, he knew that she was at the same point of no return, where thought was banished and only feeling made any sense.

The curtains around the bed were closed on two

sides, leaving only the side that faced the fireplace open. When he laid her down, candlelight glimmered across her body, and he traced the shadows with his fingers.

There was only one thing in the world that he needed to do now. He needed to make her come, as hard and as long as he could. From the way she was trembling in his arms, that wasn't going to be all that difficult.

She accepted him inside her so generously. Holding him tight, making feel as if he really were a king. Jon gritted his teeth, loving the sight and sound of her pleasure and wanting to make it last. Almost afraid of the moment when she might lose control in his arms, and whether he could hold her tightly enough to reassure her.

But Chloe wasn't afraid. She wound her legs around his waist, tilting her hips towards him, taking him deeper. He saw her eyes darken suddenly as the pupils dilated even further, and she moved against him. When he took up her rhythm, her body seemed to almost hum with pleasure.

The further he pushed her, the more she responded to him. The more she responded, the stronger he became. When she came, her body arching under his, it felt as if he was being dragged down with her in the massive undertow of her pleasure.

Then suddenly everything changed. He lost his bearings, knowing only that the point of no way back was some way behind him now. His self-control slipped away. Everything slipped away, and he didn't even think to miss it because Chloe was there. When she smiled at him, her fingers digging into his back, he came so hard that he almost blacked out.

CHAPTER FOURTEEN

CHLOE WOKE, LUXURIATING in the feel of Jon's body curled around hers. When she opened her eyes she found him propped up on the pillows, cradling her in his arms, his body bathed in candlelight.

'How long have I been asleep?'

'An hour. It's still early.' His eyes held all the promise of a long night that was still ahead of them.

'Were you watching me?' If she'd known, she would have kept her eyes closed for another couple of minutes just to feel herself under his gaze.

He smiled. 'I'm taking my duties seriously.'

'Your *duties*?' She reached up, tracing her finger across his lips. 'What duties?'

'Oh, you know. All-purpose mascot. Lucky charm.' He nodded towards the citrine, her gold chain curled around it on the dresser. 'Are you all right?'

'Better than just all right. My toes are still tingling.'

How quickly things changed. There were nights that she'd lain in bed, agonising about whether her toes were tingling or not. The power of suggestion was enough to set anyone's toes tingling if you thought about it hard enough, but Chloe had been unable to ignore it. But all that had been driven into the past now by the delicious tingle that was the aftermath of his touch.

'And that would be a good tingle?'

'Yes. A very good one.'

He bent to kiss her. 'I was thinking…'

'Yes?' She wanted to hear every last thing he was thinking. The warm curve of his lips told her that right now there wasn't a bad thought in his head.

'Seems a terrible shame to waste that bed upstairs. A glass of wine under the stars…'

'It does, doesn't it?'

The first time they'd make love had been a little uncertain, venturing onto new ground with all the excited tremor of discovery. With the second time came a sudden realisation that the first hadn't been the kind of one-time experience that couldn't be repeated. When they woke early, and Jon made love to her yet again, it was a return to that blissful place where only they existed. Lost in each other but knowing that his smile was the only compass she needed.

They were on the road a little later than they'd anticipated. He'd held her close in the bright glow of dawn. Breakfast in bed, hot chocolate and croissants, couldn't be rushed when it was eaten with Jon, and neither could the steaming bathtub, big enough to take them both.

But the road beckoned. As Jon settled into the driver's seat of his car, he quirked his lips downwards. She felt it too. Last night had been special, but they were leaving now.

'Back to reality, then.' He twisted the key in the ignition. 'You know where we're going?'

Chloe reached forward, taking the folded map from the glove compartment. She knew exactly where they were going.

* * *

The cabin could only be reached by walking through the woods. No roads, no other buildings. Just the sound of their feet on the mud path and a flock of geese, squabbling on the lake.

'How on earth did you find this place?' Chloe hadn't said where they were staying tonight, and Jon hadn't asked, but her air of excited anticipation had told him she had something up her sleeve. When they'd drawn up at the farmhouse he'd thought that this would be an idyllic place to spend the night, but the place they were actually headed to was beyond all his expectations.

'We came to stay here for three weeks one summer when I was a child. Marie-Christine and I were the same age and we made friends. We've kept in touch ever since.' The young woman who'd welcomed them had greeted Chloe with a hug and a kiss, and they'd linked arms, talking together as the three of them walked past the stable block, converted for holiday lets, and across the fields to the edge of the wood.

'They don't advertise the cabin for let. It's just for friends and family.' I gave Marie-Christine a call and she said we could have it for tonight. It was a piece of luck.'

'It's fantastic. I didn't think you could find anywhere quite as special as the chateau, but you proved me wrong.' In truth, anywhere that Chloe allowed him to lie next to her was special.

'I thought about what you said—about pacing myself.'

He put his arm around her shoulders, feeling the soft rhythm of her body against his. 'And this is you pacing yourself? Give me a call when you decide to go into overdrive.'

She chuckled. 'I love this place. Holds a lot of happy memories.'

'Your father brought you here, but he never took you to his home?' They only had another hundred miles to drive tomorrow before they reached the village where Hannah was staying.

'No, he never did. I never really thought about it, growing up. He never spoke all that much about his childhood, and you know how it is when you're a kid. You just accept what you're told and don't think to ask.'

'But Hannah wants to know where he came from?'

'I want to know too. I used to think about it a lot after my parents died but life kind of took over. There was Hannah to look after and my studies and then I became ill. It all became swallowed up.'

'But now Hannah and you have some time to explore.'

'Maybe. I hope so.' She opened the door of the cabin. One large room served as a kitchen, dining room and sitting room. 'It's just this room and two bedrooms. There's no electricity and you have to pump whatever water you need.'

'And you cook outside on the barbeque?' He gestured towards the large double barbeque built under the eaves of the cabin.

'Yes. Or if it's raining, we can go to the farmhouse.'

'Or get some bread and cheese. Fresh fruit and a bottle of wine…' He put their bags down on the floor, folding his arms around her shoulders. 'Just the two of us.'

'That sounds so good.' Her fingers traced fire across his chest, bringing back exquisite memories of last night and the promise of another, just as explosively sweet.

'So…' She glanced at the two doors at the far end of the main room. 'Which bedroom are we going to start with?'

They'd travelled three hundred miles in three days. And Chloe felt as if she'd stepped away from her life, surfacing from all the worries and pain that had submerged her and finally taking a deep breath. Perhaps the first since her parents had died.

If she'd made this journey on her own she would have covered the distance, but she would have brought along most of the old familiar baggage. But with Jon that was impossible. It wasn't just the sex, which left her unable to think about anything other than his touch and the urgent need to keep breathing, just so she could feel it again. It was him. Sitting with him in the car, feeling the miles roll by. Eating with him. Talking with him, when there was nothing much to say but they both wanted to hear the other's voice.

And now, driving through the village that spread lazily across the landscape, as if it were basking in the afternoon sun, she felt like a child, pressing her face against the car window, anxious to see everything. In truth, it was unremarkable, not particularly pretty but not completely ugly either. If it had been any other place she would have let it just slip by, but she gazed at every shop in the main street, each café, everyone who walked along the pavement, because any one of them over about fifty might have known her father.

'That woman…' She indicated a woman with a baby buggy outside the small supermarket, whose mid-brown hair was about the same colour as her own. 'She could be a second or third cousin, for all I know.'

He left her to her speculations. Wondering if her

father had climbed the old chestnut tree in the village square. Whether he'd gone to the café, which looked as if it had been there for ever, with his parents. Her grandparents, the ones who looked like strangers in the photographs.

'Did your father have brothers and sisters?'

'No, he was an only child. His mother died just before my parents married.'

'And his father?'

'Apparently he left her. I don't know why, Dad never used to talk about him. He wasn't from around here.'

'And your parents met here?'

'Yes. My mother was doing a gap year before going to art college. She ended up here for a couple of nights on the way somewhere else, and met my father. She decided to stay a week and then…that was it, really. When she came back to England my dad came with her, and after that they always lived there, although they both loved France and came back here as often as they could. Not here, though. I wish I knew why.'

'There might not be any particular reason. I don't go back to my home town all that much.'

'There's a reason for that, isn't there?' The bitterness of his divorce. The way his family had chosen to support his ex-wife and not him.

'I suppose there is.' His brow creased, and it seemed that Jon didn't want to talk about it. 'Where did Hannah say to go?'

'Through the village.' Hannah had told them that she would be away from the village for a day or so but back on Saturday, and that she'd book two rooms for them at the boarding house where she was staying.

They found the place, a neat, whitewashed house at the older and prettier end of the village. Chloe followed

Jon inside, watching as he used a mixture of signs and broken French to indicate that he wanted one double room, not two singles. Chloe didn't step in. It was nice that he'd just done it, without having to refer to her at all. That there was no longer any question about whether they were together.

Their room was quiet and unremarkable. Pale walls and pale fabrics, with dark wooden furniture that didn't quite match but went well enough together. Jon put their bags down on the bed and Chloe stared at them, sitting together. It was almost as if she'd brought someone home to introduce him to her parents, and she half expected them to burst through the door, her mother taking her to one side to put her father's glowering disapproval over booking just one room into a gentler, more persuasive form.

But she was a grown up now. She'd managed for ten years alone, and her parents would surely have respected whatever decision she made about sleeping arrangements.

'Would you like to go and look around the village?' He planted his hands on the deep window sill, looking out of the window. 'There's a church over there, we could take a stroll in that direction.'

'Could we...? Would you mind if we waited for Hannah? Knowing her, she's likely to have a full itinerary of my father's every move, right from when he was born to when he left here. When she gets a bee in her bonnet she gets very single-minded.'

'And you don't want to take a little look yourself first?' His easygoing smile said that it really didn't matter one way or the other.

'I think I'd like Hannah to show me. You know, I've realised that most of the things she knows about Mum and Dad are from when she was young, or what James and I have told her. She's never had anything that she can tell us.'

He nodded. 'That sounds like a nice idea. And, of course, if Hannah's telling the story, then it might give you more of a clue about what she's really doing here.'

'Yes. I thought that too.' She walked over to the window, laying one hand on his shoulder, and he turned and kissed her. Strong and yet so gentle. There for her, giving her his thoughts on things, without telling her what to do.

'Thank you, Jon.'

'What for?' He chuckled suddenly, hugging her tight. 'On second thoughts, I'll be expecting very full recompense. For all these things you seem to think I've done.'

'And what would that be?' She traced her finger across his lips. She had a good idea, and it would be her pleasure.

'I think… Maybe we take a walk in the garden. Have a cup of tea. Then we can come back here and you can take your dress off. As slowly as you like.'

'And then?' Chloe could dispense with the cup of tea.

'We take a shower. Go out and find some dinner.'

'Aren't you missing something?' She flipped the top button of his shirt open and he kissed her again. This time harder, a first step on the road that would take them into each other's arms.

'Probably.' His smile turned wolfish. No one smiled like that at the thought of a walk in the garden and a cup of tea. 'Want to take me through it? In detail?'

CHAPTER FIFTEEN

JON WASN'T SURE that his body could take much more of this. In the months after his marriage had ended and, if the truth be told, for some while before it had ended he'd been unable to work up any enthusiasm for sex. He'd been going through the motions with Helen, hoping that things would get better, and that she wasn't feeling quite so empty inside as he was, but when they'd split up it had been almost a relief that the physical side of things was now at an end.

Since then, there had been a couple of affairs. Consenting adults, no strings, that kind of thing. Where both parties knew exactly what they were doing, and how it was going to end. But although he and Chloe had both gone into this with their eyes open, and it wasn't such a different arrangement, it felt as if it were spinning wildly out of control.

And the thing was, he couldn't stop it. Couldn't help wanting her, every minute of the day. Not just her touch but her sweetness and her strength. Her unpredictability, the times she was wrong, and the times she was right. The way that they seemed so different in so many ways but that together they somehow managed to fit perfectly.

And that wasn't the worst of it. Frequent sex—he could handle that. The kind of sex that didn't feel that burning heat, or sweat, or ragged, incoherent cries were incongruous and should be avoided—he could most definitely handle that. But lying in her arms in the soft darkness, knowing that he'd been broken, was different. Watching one tear trickle from the corner of Chloe's eye, knowing that it wasn't joy or pain but a sign that she had given herself as completely as he had... That was entirely different.

It would cool. Everything cooled at some point and he and Chloe were so different that the cracks would appear soon enough. When Hannah arrived, they would have something else to think about, rather than just the road and each other.

He sat with her on a bench in the bus station, feeling the warm pressure of her body leaning against his. If this was the beginning of the end, it was partly a relief, wholly regrettable, but it was the way things were and he couldn't fight it.

'She said...' Chloe watched as a bus drew up in one of the bays, the doors opening and people starting to get out. 'There must be another bus coming at this time. That can't be the one.'

Probably not. The people getting out of the bus were chatting and laughing amongst themselves, obviously having made friendships. They looked good company, but no one was under fifty, which wasn't the age group that he would have expected Hannah to naturally gravitate towards.

'Well, I never...' Jon followed Chloe's pointing finger and saw Hannah climb down from the bus. Her rucksack was one of the first bags out of the luggage compartment and she collected it, laughing with the couple who were standing next to her as the man teased her about something.

'What's Hannah doing on a silver surfers' bus trip?' Jon couldn't see anything wrong with the people standing around the bus, but he reckoned that Hannah would dismiss them, labelling them as boring.

'No idea.' Chloe stood up, waving to Hannah, and she bade a cheery goodbye to her companions, walking over to them.

Chloe had obviously thought about this and knew exactly what she was going to do. No running at Hannah, no frantic grabbing at her, no tears. She spread her arms, smiling as Hannah gave her a hug and a kiss, and then let her go.

'How's Amy?' Chloe had told him that when Hannah called, those were always the first words from her mouth.

'I called James this morning and she's fine. It's good to see you. You look so well...' Chloe kept hold of Hannah's hand. She did look well, less pale than when she'd been with James in Cornwall. And she'd dyed her hair a lighter, more natural colour, rather than the black that she usually favoured.

'You too.' Hannah grinned at Chloe, and turned her attention to Jon. 'Thanks for coming.'

This was something new too. Whenever he'd seen Hannah with James she'd always been the kid sister. But from the way she put her arm around Chloe's shoulders, it seemed that Hannah had developed a protective streak for her sister. She'd grown up a little.

'My pleasure. We drove down. Had a few days' holiday.'

'Yeah?' Hannah raised her eyebrows. 'That's good.'

'So did you enjoy the coach trip?' Chloe ventured the question.

'Yeah, actually. It was only two days, and I wanted

to take in a bit of the history of the area, so I booked it. I thought it was going to be dreadful when I saw that lot.' Hannah jerked her thumb over her shoulder at her fellow travellers. 'But it was so interesting. One of the guys on the trip is a history teacher— well, he was before he retired—and he really made it all come alive. And his wife's an absolute darling. So funny.'

'Good.' Chloe kept her thoughts to herself over Hannah's abrupt volte face over whether anyone over twenty-five had anything to offer. 'Shall we go back to the boarding house? Then maybe you can show me around a bit.'

'You haven't checked the village out?'

'No, I wanted you to show me.' Chloe had clearly decided that she was going to leave the more difficult questions for later, and for now just watch and wait. It was an approach that Jon reckoned was wholly right.

'Oh, okay, then.' Hannah seemed pleased at the thought. 'Have you got the car with you, or do we need to grab a bus back to the village?'

Jon had let them talk, strolling beside them, hands in pockets as if he was just there for the scenery. But he was there. It made her feel strong enough to wait, to let Hannah dictate the pace.

They dropped Hannah's rucksack at the boarding house and walked into the centre of the village to get some lunch. Hannah had brought a blue plastic folder with her, and from the way she put it on the table next to her, it held something important. Chloe was dreading the moment when Hannah decided to show her what was inside it.

'When you said you were driving, I thought you might be planning to throw a blanket over my head and tie me up. Take me back home.' One of the things that Chloe liked about Hannah was that she didn't beat about the bush. It was sometimes brutal, but at least it was honest.

Although she wasn't quite sure that she knew the answer to this. *No, I wasn't* sounded as if she didn't care. *Yes, I was* wasn't much of a reassurance that she was here to listen and learn.

'I talked Chloe out of it.' Jon seemed to have woken suddenly from his reverie. 'She might not care about losing her licence to practise after being brought up on kidnapping charges, but I do.'

Chloe shot him a silent *thank you* and Hannah grinned. 'So I'm not going to need the pepper spray to defend myself?'

Maybe Hannah was joking and maybe not. Jon smiled. 'That rather depends on what you're defending yourself from.'

He went back to his meal and the matter was dropped. When the waitress brought coffee, Hannah reached for the folder. 'I want to show you… I found some things out. About Dad.'

Chloe breathed a sigh of relief. The nagging fear that perhaps there had been legal papers in the folder, something that formalised Hannah's intention to leave Amy behind, was unfounded. 'Show me. I'd love to see.'

Hannah opened the folder on the first page. A black and white map of the village, a few of the buildings coloured in by hand. 'This is where Dad lived. In blue. And the mauve is where our grandmother was born.'

Chloe leaned over the map. 'Right here? By the village green?'

'Yes, her parents had a shop.' Hannah's face had the

intent look she got when she had hold of something and wasn't letting go. 'Haberdashery.'

Hannah leaned over, flipping through the pages, finding the right one. The photograph was a copy of an older one, the creases showing up on the print. 'Who's that standing outside?'

'Guess.' Hannah's face was flushed with triumph.

'I don't know. The proprietor…our great-grandfather?' Chloe peered at the figure. She could hardly make any features out, just a man in a white apron standing in the shadow of the doorway. He looked as if he had a moustache.

'Yes.'

'Wow.' Chloe looked at the photograph again. 'Where did you get this? You've done it all in the last week?'

'No, I've been working on it for a while, using the internet, but coming here everything fell into place. The *pasteur* at the church gave me the photo. His predecessor had a thing about the village history and he collected a load of things and catalogued them all. It's all still kept up at the church, along with the parish records.'

'But…' The nagging doubt that there was something wrong with the photograph suddenly resolved into certainty. 'The shopfront. It says *Delancourt*. That wasn't our grandmother's name, was it?'

Hannah laughed. 'Wondered when you'd notice. When Dad's father left, she reverted back to her maiden name. And Dad took her name, because he didn't want anything to do with his father.'

Chloe stole a glance at Jon. Families breaking up, not wanting anything to do with each other. If the subject was a sore spot for him, he wasn't showing it.

'Why did Dad do that?'

'His father beat them.'

'How on earth do you know that?'

'The pastor at the church put me in touch with someone who knew Dad. They were at school together. I went
and talked to him.'

Sadness suddenly struck Chloe. This was all fas-
cinating, but Hannah had left her own child to chase
people who were long dead. She asked the question as
gently as she could.

'This is why you left? To find out about our dad?'
Chloe swallowed down the impulse to be cross with
Hannah. Surely this was no reason to abandon Amy.

The light died in Hannah's eyes. 'No, I…'

'Sometimes, when you can't make sense of the present, it helps to try and make sense of the past. Because
the past is over and done with and can't hurt you.' Jon
spoke suddenly, his voice gentle.

Hannah's eyes began to blur with tears. 'I'm sorry,
Chloe.'

'It's okay. You did the best you could, Hannah, and
you made sure that Amy was safe.' Chloe was beginning to see that maybe Hannah had done the only thing
she could do. Something was very wrong, and she'd
been trying to protect Amy from that. She reached for
her sister's hand, holding it tight.

Hannah was retreating fast, her face taking on that
look of dumb watchfulness that Chloe had seen so many
times before. They had to stop now. She glanced at Jon
and the ghost of a nod told her that he understood.

'May I look at your photos, please, Hannah?' He
slid his hand across the table towards the blue folder.

Hannah nodded, and Jon started to leaf through the
pages, asking questions and complimenting Hannah on
what she'd found out. Slowly Hannah began to emerge

from her shell and started to talk fluently. It seemed that this project was her way of making sense of something.

'And all the births and marriages of the Delancourt family are in the church records?' Jon was examining the family tree that Hannah had drawn up.

'Most of them. I'll show you. And we can go to the churchyard as well. Our grandmother's buried there. And guess what her name is.'

Chloe shrugged. 'I don't know. I can't remember Dad ever mentioning it.'

'*Flora* Delancourt.'

Jon looked questioningly at Chloe's smile. 'My middle name's Flora.' The more she thought about it the more she liked having her grandmother's name. 'That's so nice, Hannah. That he called me after her.'

Hannah was grinning too. 'Yeah. I think so too.'

Jon's fingers touched Chloe's arm. She followed his gaze across the road and nodded, turning to Hannah. 'Can we take flowers? There's a florist over there, we could get some.'

'Yeah. I think that would be great.'

It had been a long day. They had gone to the church, and then Hannah had walked them around the village, more than once if the familiarity of some of the land marks and houses wasn't just *déjà vu*.

After dinner, Jon had gone back to their room, making an excuse to leave them alone to talk. As soon as he was out of earshot Hannah had turned to her.

'Well?'

It was the question that Chloe had been dreading, because she'd been asking it of herself for the last few days and hadn't come up with a satisfactory answer. What on earth *was* she doing?

'Good question.'

Hannah leaned back in her seat in the deserted sitting room. 'Which you're not going to answer. Jon told me that you weren't an item.'

'Well, we weren't at that point. It all just…happened. It's not serious.'

Hannah pulled a face. 'Of course it isn't serious. It's been…what, three days? Nothing's serious after three days.'

It felt like a lot longer. It felt as if somehow she'd known Jon her whole life, without actually knowing him. 'Yes, but this… Neither of us have any intention of making it serious in the future.'

A slow smile spread across Hannah's face. 'So…? Friends with benefits?'

'No!' Actually, Hannah had hit the nail pretty squarely on the head, even if there were some important differences. Surely friends with benefits didn't spend most of the day thinking about each other.

'What, then?'

'Okay. It's probably friends with benefits.' That was the closest she could get to explaining it in a few words, even if it didn't cover the feeling that Jon had broken her and then re-made her into someone who was slightly different.

'Shame. He's nice. He'd be good for you. Jake was a creep, leaving you like that.'

'What?' Chloe had never said anything about Jake to Hannah. She'd tried to protect her from the more awkward facts of life, and there had been a few things she hadn't mentioned.

Hannah pressed her lips together. 'I know what you were doing. I was only a kid and you kept all that to yourself. It was pretty obvious, though. You got ill and he walked out.'

This had to stop. And Chloe had to be the one to stop it because Hannah needed to release some of the secrets that seemed to be eating her up. She leaned forward, taking Hannah's hand.

'There's a lot we haven't said to each other, Hannah. But the trouble with secrets is that you hug them close and they come back and smack you in the face.'

Hannah raised her eyebrows. 'Jake smacked you in the face?'

'Not literally.' A few months—just a few weeks ago Chloe wouldn't have been able to bring herself to talk about this. It was an uncomfortable reminder that Jon really *had* changed her.

'Look, Hannah. I was very ill, and I still worry about ever being that way again, even if I do know that it's not going to happen. And I felt so alone when Jake dumped me. I wanted to protect you from all of that but it was wrong of me not to say anything and I'm really sorry for that.'

'It's okay. I did know.'

'Yes, and if we'd discussed it, I could have told you it was okay. It was hard, and I felt dreadful, but in the end I was determined that I'd get through it. Wouldn't that have made you feel better?'

Hannah nodded silently.

Chloe took a deep breath. Jon had given her the courage to tell her own secrets, and maybe he could give her the courage to ask the same of Hannah.

'Whatever it is that's the matter, it can't hurt me, Hannah. And it can't hurt you either. If you'll tell me, I'll just listen and maybe that will help.'

CHAPTER SIXTEEN

IT WAS LATE when she got back to their room, and Chloe opened the door quietly, sure that Jon must be asleep. But the light by the bed was on and he was propped up on the pillows, reading.

'How's Hannah?' He seemed to be able to read Chloe's distress and confusion on her face.

'Sleeping. We talked quite a bit.'

He nodded. 'Can you tell me about it?'

'Yes.' Chloe sat down on the bed next to him. It seemed that tonight he'd made some kind of decision, because even though the evening had been warm he was wearing an old T-shirt, the bedcovers pulled over his legs. It seemed strange not to find him naked in their bed.

'Do you *want* to tell me about it?'

Yes. More than anything. 'I told her about what happened with me and Jake, and how I felt I'd let her down. She told me some things about Amy's father. I thought that there was no contact between them after she came home, but she texted him and told him she was pregnant.'

'What was his reaction?' The look in Jon's eyes told her that he already had some idea.

'He said that the baby probably wasn't his anyway.

When she told him that she loved him and there hadn't been anyone else, he said that if she really loved him she'd terminate the pregnancy, and let him get on with his life.'

Jon shook his head, cursing quietly under his breath. 'If James had only known that. If *I'd* known it even…'

'Why do you think she kept quiet? James was ready to wring his neck anyway. She sent a photo when Amy was born, but he just messaged back telling her never to contact him again. She said that she felt so worthless. Perhaps that's where some of these bad feelings about herself started.'

'It wouldn't be all that surprising.' The tenderness in Jon's eyes was making her melt. 'So all the time you've been putting a brave face on things, and so has Hannah.'

'I was so quick to accept that she didn't care about him because I was trying not to care about Jake. When I told her that maybe she should just let him go, I thought I was giving her my honest opinion, but maybe it was just what I thought *I* should do.'

'It was good advice. I don't see that Hannah would have benefited by having him in her life.'

'Thanks. But I know what I've done wrong.'

'She really *is* better off without him. And so is Amy.'

He reached for her and Chloe shifted towards him on the bed so that he could fold her in his arms. Chloe wanted to just curl up with him, but the bedclothes were in the way. Surely friends with benefits only wanted to be close for the good times, not the bad.

'Thank you. For being here.'

'I just drove.'

She dug her elbow into his ribs. Or where she reckoned his ribs must be under the T-shirt and the duvet. 'No, you didn't. I don't think I would have had the courage to try and break through with Hannah if you hadn't been here. And I know it must have been hard for you.'

'Me? I don't—' He broke off as Chloe reached up, putting her finger over his lips.

'If you're going to tell me that none of this is hard for you, you can save your breath.'

'Yeah, okay. It's hard. You and Hannah and James are all so close and…to be honest, I don't think any of my family would even notice if I went missing, let alone come and find me.'

'I'll find you.' Chloe started to peel away the layers of bedclothes that were wrapped around him.

'Hey. Don't you want to sleep?' He broke off, groaning as Chloe's hand found its way inside his boxer shorts.

'No. I want to let go of the past. Don't you?'

He levered his body over hers, rolling her backwards on the bed and pinning her down. 'Yes, I do. I want to promise you…whatever you want.'

She knew he was sincere, even if he was struggling with the idea. He *did* want to let go of the past and promise her at least a part of his future. But she couldn't ask him to do it. Asked-for promises didn't work.

'Don't promise me anything, Jon. This is what I want. Exactly this.'

'You're sure?'

She pulled him down for a kiss. His kisses held nothing back and promised her everything. 'I just want you to make love to me.'

He smiled down at her, tenderness in his face. 'Take your clothes off, sweetheart.'

He loved watching Chloe undress, and she knew it. When she came to him, all of Jon's resolve, every last bit of his determination to let her just sleep tonight was shattered into tiny pieces.

This time broke the mould yet again. They'd already spent more time than they might reasonably have been expected to spare over the last three days in learning each other's bodies. And each time they'd found some new way of giving each other pleasure.

But when Chloe came to him, stripping off his T-shirt and boxer shorts, all he wanted to do was hold her. Be close to her in every way. Their lovemaking was tender, a reminder of good things when there were so many difficulties threatening, and it touched Jon more deeply than he'd thought possible.

Afterwards, feeling her curled up in the curve of his body, he held her close.

'Chloe…?'

'Hmm?' She snuggled up against him, winding her hand around his, kissing his fingers. It answered all of the questions he wanted to ask.

'Go to sleep, sweetheart. Tomorrow's another day.'

Over the next few days they did all the things that tourists might. Driving to a local chateau that was open to the public, taking a picnic out into the countryside. Chloe and Hannah spent a lot of time talking, sometimes with Jon there and sometimes on their own, and slowly Hannah was beginning to open up.

'Are we going home?' Jon lay in bed, last night's lovemaking still tingling through his senses, watching Chloe brush her hair in the morning sunlight.

'I think so. If that's all right with you. How did you know?'

'You were muttering in your sleep last night.' Chloe

had come to bed late and fallen asleep almost immediately in his arms.

'Was I?' She turned to face him. 'What did I say?'

'Just a few words. Home was one of them.' His name
had been another. He'd loved it that she'd cried out for
him, even in her sleep.

'Hannah's agreed to come back with us, whenever
we're ready to go. She's going to stay with me for a
while, along with Amy.'

'And you'll see how things go?'

Chloe shook her head. 'No, we're not leaving things
to chance. I'm going to sort out someone for Hannah to
talk to and work things through with. I'll go along too,
if there are issues that we need to work out together.'

'That sounds like a good plan. So Hannah will be
taking over the spare room.'

'There's always room for you. You'd have to sleep
with me, though, if that's not too onerous for you.' She
smiled at him.

'I'll put a brave face on it. And when you get tired
of me, my own place has a bathroom now. The builder
texted me last night.'

There was an uncertainty about all this. They were
covering it up well with jokes and smiles, but there
was a slight tremor to Chloe's tone, which matched the
tremor in his heart. They knew how to make love, but
neither was quite sure how they fitted into each other's lives.

A knock sounded on the door, along with Hannah's
voice. Jon got out of bed, pulling on a pair of jeans and
a T-shirt, and Chloe called for her to come in.

'Have you told him?' Hannah dispensed with the
usual 'Good morning'. She was obviously looking for-

ward to going home with Chloe, and that had to be a good thing.

'I hear that you're coming back with us. And you'll be staying with Chloe for a while.' Jon grinned at her.

'Yes.' Hannah's smile was radiant, excited, as if this was a new beginning. For her, it was, and her future seemed more assured than his did right now. 'When can we go?'

'We haven't got round to that yet,' Chloe rebuked her gently. So much had changed between the two sisters. They voiced their own wants and needs more freely, no longer afraid to negotiate something that suited them both.

But it was obvious that they were both looking forward to going home. 'We could go today, if you want.'

'Today?' Hannah grinned. 'That's fine with me.'

'Me too.' Chloe looked at Jon. 'Shall I see if I can book a hotel for us? About halfway?'

Suddenly he wanted this done with. To stop worrying about what would happen between him and Chloe when they got home, and just get there. 'Or if you can book a channel crossing for late this afternoon, we could do it in a day. It's still early, and if we're packed and ready to go in an hour…'

Chloe was biting her lip. Perhaps she was as afraid of this as he was. In which case it was better to do it now, before the uncertainty began to gnaw at them both.

'Yes.' She seemed to come to the same conclusion he had. 'We'll do that, then.'

They shared the driving, eating in the car, and made the channel crossing just in time. Hitting the Friday evening traffic as they approached London slowed them down and it was late when Jon drew up outside Chloe's house. Carrying their bags in, they dropped them in the hall.

Chloe seemed on edge, bustling around, opening windows and doors to air the house and then closing them again when the chill evening breeze made her shiver. She switched the kettle on for tea, even though no one wanted it. And the one question that seemed to be on everyone's mind—who was going to sleep where—needed to be answered soon because they were all tired.

In the end, Hannah made the first move, fetching her sleeping bag from where it was tied securely to the top of her rucksack, and laying it on the sofa. 'I'm ready to turn in.'

'Why don't you take the spare room? It'll only take a minute for me to clear my things out, and I can sleep down here.' Jon saw Chloe raise her eyebrows and his heart jumped suddenly. Maybe she did want him in her bed still.

Hannah looked from Jon to Chloe and then back again. Then she rolled her eyes, grabbing her rucksack and stomping up the stairs. Jon could hear her banging around in the spare room, and when she came back downstairs she had the few clothes that he hadn't packed and taken to France with him bundled in her arms.

'Here.' She dropped them onto the sofa and picked up her sleeping bag. 'Work it out, people. I'm going to bed.'

Jon heard Chloe giggle behind him. Then he felt her wrap her arms around his waist, her body pressing against his back. 'I'm sorry. I think she gets the unsubtle streak from James.'

Jon turned. It was the first time he'd held her today, and he hadn't realised how much he'd missed it. It felt like a long, deep breath after hours of fighting for air. 'Don't knock it. It's one of the things I like about James.'

'Me too.' She looked up at him, her gaze melting through his uncertainty. 'Would you come to mine?'

He kissed her forehead. 'I'd like that very much.'

Coming home was so full of promise. A new start for Hannah, this time based on firmer foundations. And so full of questions where Jon was concerned. They'd made no promises and told no lies. The only plan they had was that there was no plan. But reality demanded that they make one, sooner or later.

Not tonight, though. He led her up the stairs and she closed the door of her bedroom behind them. Jon pulled his sweater and shirt off over his head in one movement, and she remembered how much she loved his body. So strong, bulky in all the right places, and yet his eyes were so tender. His arms so warm.

And he knew just what she needed. Tonight was no exception to that. His nakedness was somehow innocent, rather than sexual, as he slipped between the sheets, waiting for her to undress and come to bed.

'What's going to happen now?' It felt as if everything was changing and the only thing she could cling to was him.

'Go to sleep, sweetheart.' He curled his body around hers, holding her. 'We'll work it out in the morning.'

There was no time to work it out in the morning. A call from Jon's builder took him off to his house to decide on what should be done about a leak in the roof that had become apparent after heavy rain a few days ago, and he didn't return until after lunch. By that time, she and

Hannah were getting ready to go to the supermarket and restock the fridge.

'I'll go.' Hannah took her car keys out of her hand.

'No, it's okay…' Making a big thing of this was only going to make things worse. Chloe had spent the whole morning wondering what Jon was going to do next, and she needed to calm down.

'I'll be back this time. Promise.' Hannah kissed her on the cheek and grinned at Jon, then picked up the shopping bags, slamming the front door behind her.

'How's your roof?'

He shrugged. 'Not great. I spent all morning up in the loft, plugging holes. I think I'll have to get the roofers in to renew the back elevation.'

'You look very clean. Your loft obviously isn't as dusty as mine.'

'After the builder went, I tried out the new shower.'

It seemed like one more hole in a structure that was already rapidly disintegrating. Jon was showering at his place now. Chloe told herself not to be stupid. Of course he wanted to use his new bathroom.

'How was it?'

'Good. Great, actually.'

The time was now. Hannah would be gone for at least an hour and they could talk. Work out what happened next. The thought occurred to her that if neither of them cared, they could have avoided this, just letting things slide and walking away. On the other hand, if they both cared enough, that would have been obvious too, and they would have known what to do next without having to talk about it.

'Let's go and sit down.' He walked into the sitting room and Chloe followed him, sitting down in the chair opposite his.

'Jon, I...' Now that the time had come, she didn't know what she wanted to say.

'Chloe, there's nothing that we have to do. Nothing we can't do.' He'd obviously been thinking about this a little more cogently than she had. 'But you have big changes ahead of you and so do I, for that matter.'

'Does that really matter? Life never just stops.'

'No, but we'll both be busy. Maybe we should take a break and think about things. We don't need to make any decisions or promises, just wait a bit until everything settles.'

A glimmer of what was really going on in Jon's head. Just a few days ago it had seemed that they could both read each other's minds effortlessly, but now it was a guessing game. But she knew that he'd been burned like this before, he and his wife drifting apart because of schedules that never included enough time for each other.

Suddenly, it was all very clear. The last few weeks had left them with no option. They'd been so close, not just physically but emotionally as well. They'd supported each other, worked as a team. Loved each other. There had been no need for promises, the commitment had been made.

'Jon, I think I need to tell you where I stand. We're either in a relationship or we aren't. I want to be in a relationship with you, but if that's not possible then I think we should just call it a day. I don't want an on-off affair.'

He stared at her. 'We said—'

'I don't care what we said. That's what I want. I love you and I think we could make a go of it. But I need you to tell me that you love me too, and that you'll be there for me.'

'I do love you, Chloe, but...' He got to his feet and

started to pace. 'I won't just jump in blindly when neither of us is going to have the time or the energy to really make this work. We need to think about it.'

'I don't. I can't, Jon. I've been let down too many times.'

He turned suddenly, his face dark. 'Did I ever let you down?'

'No, that's not what I'm saying. I'm just telling you how I feel.'

'And what about how *I* feel. Don't I get a say in this?'

'Yes, of course you do. You stay or you go.' Chloe felt tears pricking at the sides of her eyes and blinked them back. All the anger and frustration that was battering them seemed to have come out of nowhere.

'All or nothing, you mean. That's crazy, Chloe, we've known each other three weeks.'

'No, I mean something or nothing. I don't want you to just turn up whenever you feel like a one-night stand and can't be bothered to flip through your address book.' Chloe bit her tongue. She hadn't meant that…

'I'm going to pretend you didn't say that, Chloe. Because if you think that's all you've been to me you're wrong.' He didn't give her a chance to tell him that she was sorry and that the words had come out of nowhere. Jon marched out of the room, stomping upstairs.

He grabbed his shaving kit from the bathroom, throwing it into the holdall that wasn't fully unpacked yet from yesterday. Sorting through the washing basket, separating her things from his, he tried not to notice that her scent still clung to his clothes, like a bittersweet memory.

The worst thing about it was that she was right. Chloe had been hurt badly, at a time when she'd most needed love and care, and it just wasn't fair to expect her to continue a relationship without the security of knowing that he'd be there for her when she needed him.

But Jon couldn't do that. Not yet, and maybe not ever. The thought of building something together and then watching it disintegrate, under the pressure of time and other commitments, was too much for him to bear.

The old feeling, that this was the way of things and that any relationship would cool given enough time, reasserted itself. His and Chloe's may have burned a little hotter, but that just meant that it was more difficult when the flame was extinguished.

He zipped the holdall and straightened up, stopping for a moment to make sure he'd packed everything because he knew he wouldn't be back. Then he walked back downstairs.

Chloe was standing in the kitchen doorway. It looked as if she'd been crying.

'I'm sorry. I didn't mean what I said.'

He stayed at the bottom of the stairs. If he went any closer he might not be able to do this.

'You meant it, Chloe. And you're absolutely right. I meant what I said, too.'

She stood stock still. 'And what you need from a relationship is pretty much the exact opposite of what I need.'

'Yes.' Finally they agreed, but it was the last thing he wanted to agree over. He turned for the front door.

'Jon... Wait.'

When he looked back, he saw that she had her hand over her mouth in disbelief, tears running down her cheeks. And that look in her eyes, the one he knew so well, told him all he needed to know.

'I know. I love you too. That's why I have to go.'

He opened the front door and found Hannah standing right in front of him, searching in her bag for her keys. He gave her a nod, silently thanking the heavens above that she was back so soon, and slid past her, walking down the front path to his car.

'What the blazes…?' Hannah left the shopping on the front doorstep and rushed forward, enveloping Chloe in a hug. 'What did he do?'

'Nothing. He didn't do anything.' Chloe blew her nose on a piece of kitchen roll. 'We… It was never going to work out. We both knew that, and… It's okay. I'm okay.'

'No, you aren't.' Hannah marched back to the door and picked up the shopping. 'But you will be. I've got the very thing.'

She took a tub of chocolate-chip ice cream from the bag, and Chloe smiled, despite herself. 'I don't need that.' At the moment she felt that she didn't need anything, other than Jon, but that would pass.

'Do me a favour, would you, and let me be the big sister for a change.' Hannah opened the cutlery drawer, took two spoons out and then reached up to get two glasses from the top shelf of the cabinet.

'What are they for?'

Hannah produced a bottle of red wine from the shopping bag. 'It's you, me and the sofa for the rest of the afternoon. We'll put the TV on, eat ice cream and drink wine.'

'And then we'll be sick?'

'No, we won't. Moderation's the key with this. Eat the ice cream slowly and sip the wine.'

Chloe hugged Hannah, feeling her limbs tremble as she hung onto her sister. She and Jon had done the right thing, however much it hurt. They were never going to be able to make it work. It had been wrong from the start.

She kissed Hannah's cheek. 'Okay, big sis. Let's do it.'

CHAPTER SEVENTEEN

A LOT HAD happened in the last three months. Hannah and Amy had moved in permanently with Chloe, and they'd run a whole gamut of feelings together. Crises were averted, hugs were exchanged, and new avenues and opportunities were explored. But the one thing that hadn't happened was that she'd bumped into Jon at the hospital.

She'd been almost relieved. She knew she couldn't see Jon again, not yet. The idea that they could be friends, with or without benefits, after all that had happened between them was ludicrous.

And he obviously felt the same. Chloe had kept to her side of the hospital and he'd kept to his. She'd heard a few people talk about him, and supposed he must have heard people talk about her, but she'd resisted the temptation to show any interest. His signature had been on the records for some of her patients, children who'd been referred up through A and E, and she'd even traced her finger around the loop of the *J* once or twice. But that was all.

It hurt, but it had to be done. She'd get over it. It was just a matter of when.

Even so, the early morning call from A and E made her hesitate. But there was a patient there with a displaced ankle fracture. Before he was admitted for surgery it required a recommendation from one of the doctors from Orthopaedics, and Chloe was the one who happened to be at work early this morning.

She walked down to A and E, trembling. In and out. Don't look right or left, don't stop to talk. Just do your job. With any luck Jon wouldn't be on shift this morning.

The doctor who had called beckoned her into an empty cubicle and she sat down next to him at the monitor to look at the X-rays.

'He's had a fall, but there doesn't seem to be a concussion, although we'll be keeping a close eye on that, particularly if he needs surgery. I'm reckoning he might…' Dr Marshall had worked in A and E for long enough that nothing much surprised him, and he could usually anticipate what ongoing care his patients would need.

'I'd say so.' Chloe looked carefully at the X-rays. 'That's a nasty one. I'll wait and take the paperwork upstairs with me. I can have it on Mr Saunders's desk for when he comes in.'

'I'd appreciate it. He's one of ours, he works here.'

'Well, he's not going to be at work for a while…' Chloe's eye drifted to the patient's name in the corner of the screen and her hand flew to her mouth. 'Jon?'

'Yes. He's quite new here, you might not know him…'

Never mind that. Chloe didn't have the time to think up something appropriate to explain that she knew Jon very well. 'What happened to him?'

'Apparently he was up in the loft at his house early this morning. Something gave way and his foot went through the ceiling.'

'He fell through the ceiling…' Chloe must have been showing all the signs of panic because Dr Marshall snapped into reassurance mode.

'No, he fell over. There's the damage to his ankle, and he's going to have quite a shiner tomorrow. Apparently he managed to get down from the loft and then down the stairs, trying to reach his phone. But the builders came in at six and found him in the hallway. Called an ambulance.'

'But he's okay?' Suddenly that was all that mattered. Jon had been hurt and there had been no one there to help him.

'Go and take a look for yourself. I've got to wait for the results on some routine tests and I'll be ten minutes with the paperwork….' Chloe was on her feet already and Dr Marshall called after her. 'Cubicle Six.'

His ankle was uncomfortably numb. His left eye was closing fast, and it was more than likely that he'd be staying here for a couple of days. Jon was sick of staring at the ceiling so he closed his eyes for a few moments, drifting in a sea of analgesia.

He heard the door of the cubicle open and ignored it. Probably someone wanting to take his blood pressure or check his pulse. He'd already told them that he was okay and that it was just the ankle they needed to worry about, but the A and E staff, who normally took his word for everything, had been taking it in turns to remind him that they'd be the judge of that.

'Jon…?' He felt a touch on his forehead, as light as a whisper. He must be dreaming. Jon struggled to open his eyes, since those kinds of dreams could probably get him in trouble with his work colleagues, and saw a pair of honey-brown eyes looking down at him.

'How are you?'

All he could think of was that finally someone was asking him how he felt and not telling him. And that he wanted desperately to hold onto Chloe, but that he dared not reach for her.

'Okay…' Suddenly his mouth felt as if it was full of cotton wool.

'I've taken a look at your X-rays. I think you'll need surgery to fix the bone in your ankle, but I'm putting the papers on Mr Saunders's desk as soon as I get them. He's the best, you'll be in good hands.'

She leaned over him, and he caught the scent of her soap. 'That eye looks nasty. I'll get someone to bring an ice pack. Your heart rate's slightly elevated…'

That was hardly a surprise. It had been perfectly normal before Chloe had arrived.

'Is there anything else? Any pain anywhere?'

Suddenly that didn't matter any more. 'Chloe, I'm sorry.'

She stared at him. 'What for?'

'The way I left…'

She reddened slightly, and then recovered her composure. 'We have more important things to think about—'

'No. No, this is more important.' He reached forward, trying to touch her arm, but pain shot up his leg, immobilising him.

'Hey… Hey, it's all right, Jon.' She took his hand, squeezing it.

'Please…it's not all right…' He hung on tight to her hand, trying to pull her a little closer. Chloe must have seen his anguish because she moved towards him, her free hand moving to his brow.

'What's on your mind, then?' She said the words

quietly. At last he had the opportunity that he'd been waiting for, even if this wasn't the time or the place.

'I treated you badly, Chloe. I'm so sorry.'

The pain in her eyes told him exactly how badly he'd treated her. 'We both said things that we shouldn't have. That doesn't matter any more.'

His head was clear now, as if determination to take this opportunity had overwhelmed both the pain in his leg and the effects of the analgesics in his system. 'What I said…what I *did*… It was nothing to do with you, and everything to do with me. I told you that I'd made a decision about my future after the divorce, but that wasn't entirely true. There was no decision, I was just too afraid to do anything else because I'd been too badly hurt. I've been thinking about that a lot lately.'

'You think I didn't know that?' She pursed her lips in a rueful smile. 'Anyway, I was just as much to blame as you were. I couldn't just accept it and let things alone.'

'There's no reason in the world why you should have, Chloe. I…'

She laid her finger over his lips. 'We *could* argue about who was most to blame, if it makes you feel any better. Or we could just say that neither of us wanted to be hurt, and neither of us meant to hurt. Leave it at that, eh? Let it go, because it's not what we are.'

Relief rushed through him, prompting another agonising jab of pain from his leg. Chloe had found it in that gorgeous, loving heart of hers to forgive him. And if putting the past behind them didn't change the future, it was at least a start. Jon nodded, and Chloe took her finger from his lips.

'All right. Now we've got that dealt with, you can lie still.' That schoolmistress tone that he so loved reasserted itself. 'And tell me where it hurts.'

Nothing hurt any more. Not in the light of her smile. 'They've already examined me. And there's no pain if I keep still. The ambulance paramedic gave me a shot of the good stuff.'

'What did he give you?' She snatched the notes up from the end of the bed and leafed through them. 'Okay. That looks okay.'

'Yeah. It was actually better than okay at the time.' He tried for a grin to reassure her, and must have succeeded in part because she rewarded him with a dazzling smile. All he really wanted her to do right now was to take his hand again.

'I want to take a look at your leg.' She glanced at his right ankle, which was covered over with a dressing pad, laid loosely over the top of it.

'Yes. Please do.' Jon had tried to look at the leg himself, after the paramedic had taken off his boot and cut the leg of his jeans, but gentle hands had pushed him back down, and firm voices had told him to relax. Chloe's judgement was the next best thing to his own.

She removed the dressing, tutting when she saw that it had blood on it and throwing it into surgical waste. Her touch was like the whisper of a butterfly's wing, and she bent over, looking at the ankle from one side and then the other, before tearing open a new dressing and laying it over the wound.

'Can you see the bone?'

'Yes, it's a nasty fracture, but from the X-rays, and seeing it now, it looks like a straightforward piece of surgery. It'll take a while to heal, but I don't see any reason why you can't make a full recovery.'

It was exactly what he wanted—no, needed—to hear. The unvarnished truth from someone who he trusted. *We'll get you back on your feet in no time* didn't ring true when he knew that it was beyond the wit of anyone to mend a displaced fracture that fast.

'Thanks. Chloe...'

The door of the cubicle opened and Ben Marshall leaned in. 'I've got the paperwork.'

Chloe practically tore it out of his hand and then directed a dazzling smile at him. 'Thanks. I'll take it up now.'

The thought that she was going now made Jon want to weep. Before she'd arrived he'd been coping. But now that he'd seen her face he couldn't bear to be left alone again. She walked to his bedside and he steeled himself to say one more goodbye and thank her.

'I'm just going to take these upstairs. I need to get them on Mr Saunders's desk right away. But I'll be back.'

'Thank you.' He wouldn't ask when, because maybe she'd think twice about it and not come back. And in any case, he'd be counting the hours in the hope that she did return.

'Ten minutes. I'll be ten minutes.' She took his hand, giving it a squeeze, and in that moment Jon felt completely happy.

'Don't you have patients to see?'

'My first patient's at half past nine. It's only half eight now. I'll see you in ten.' Jon nodded, and closed his eyes again. If Chloe being here was just a dream, he wanted to hold onto it for as long as he possibly could.

He didn't know how long she'd been, but from the way she was slightly out of breath it seemed that she'd been hurrying. Chloe brought an ice pack, wrapping it carefully before she laid it over his eye, and a bottle of spring water from the machine.

'Would you like something to drink?'

'Yes. Thanks.'

She nodded, opening the bottle and putting a red and white striped drinking straw into it. 'You know the drill. Small sips, okay?'

He nodded, and she held the bottle so that he could drink through the straw. Suddenly he realised he was very thirsty, but he tried to drink slowly.

'That's good. You can have a little more in a minute.' She put the bottle down beside the bed and sat down. 'I can stay for three quarters of an hour and then I have to go. But I'll come and find you again at lunchtime.'

'You don't need…' He saw the reproach in her eyes, and realised that he wanted her to come back more than anything. 'Thanks.'

She nodded. 'Whatever were you doing in the loft at six in the morning?'

Ben had told her, then. 'I heard dripping up there after last night's rain. I reckoned it was another leak and went up there just to see what was going on. One of the boards was rotten.'

She knew. Chloe knew what it was like to be alone and helpless. Far better than he did, and this morning had frightened the hell out of him. She reached forward, taking his hand, and suddenly everything was all right.

'It must have been horrible, having to try and get back downstairs.'

All he'd been able to think of had been getting downstairs to his phone before he passed out from the pain. He'd seen the blood soaking the leg of his jeans and had known he had to get help. But Chloe was here now and he could shrug it off.

'My phone was in the kitchen. I wasn't expecting the builder to come, he'd just popped in with some samples for me to look at. When he knocked, I yelled and he let himself in with his key.'

'It was a bit of luck he decided to come round. Don't you go clambering around when you're on your own in the house again.' Her voice took on the timbre of a very sexy schoolmistress.

'I've learned my lesson. May I have some more water, please?'

She reached for the water bottle and let him drink a little more. Then she sat down again, reaching for his hand. It seemed that everything that had happened between them, and the way they'd both been studiously avoiding each other for the last few months, was temporarily forgotten.

'How's Hannah? I've been thinking about her.'

'She's good. She and Amy are living with me and... well, Amy's a joy. So's Hannah. She's having counselling and starting to build up her confidence. And she's doing an Art A-Level by correspondence course. It's something she's always been interested in, and she's been producing some lovely drawings.

Even in his befuddled state, Jon could see that Chloe had changed. Or rather she'd continued on the road that he'd seen her take those first, uncertain steps on in France. She seemed so much more confident that she was doing the right thing and ready to make a success of it, for herself as well as Hannah and Amy.

'I'm glad everything turned out well, Chloe.'

'Thanks. I think you can take more than some of the credit...' She flushed red and picked up the water bottle. 'You want something more to drink?'

It seemed that she'd talked enough about the thing

that had brought them together and then torn them apart. That was okay. Jon was just glad that Chloe had come and that she'd stayed for a while. He reached for the water bottle, gasping as he moved too far and pain shot up his leg.

'Steady on. Just stay down, will you, and let me do the heavy lifting.' She gave him a smile that reached right to his heart and Jon realised that the idea that had been forming in his head for the last month wasn't just a dream. It was something that he was going to make happen.

She came back again at lunchtime, bringing a large carrier bag full of supplies. Toothpaste and a toothbrush, moist tissues for his hands and face, a few pieces of fruit and some dog-eared paperbacks from the hospital book exchange. Jon was taken down to the operating theatre late that afternoon, and when he woke up from the anaesthetic, his leg throbbing and his mouth feeling as if someone had stuffed it with cotton wool, Chloe was holding his hand.

'You should…go…' He didn't know what time it was or how long he'd been out for, but the curtains on the ward were closed and it was dark outside.

'I can stay until visiting time is over.'

She leaned forward, her fingers brushing his hair back from his brow. All he could feel was her tenderness. 'I spoke to Mr Saunders. He says that everything went well, and your leg's going to be fine. Now close your eyes and rest.'

He wanted to stay awake but the drugs in his system were dragging him back into a state of drowsy half-consciousness. The last thing he remembered was holding her hand in his, pressing it possessively against his chest.

CHAPTER EIGHTEEN

JON WOKE THE next morning to find that his eye was throbbing, his leg was in a cast, and pretty much every bone in his body ached. And there was a note from Chloe on his locker.

Today is Saturday.

Jon smiled. He'd been wondering what day it was, and Chloe had clearly anticipated that.

I'll be coming to see you this afternoon. Hannah picked some clothes up from your house yesterday and they're in your locker. If I find you've not been doing as you're told, I'll fill out the forms to have you restrained.

Jon wondered whether Hannah had broken in when she'd gone to collect his things, and decided he didn't care. Chloe was coming, and she could threaten him with whatever she liked. He needed to get out of bed.

He leaned over, reaching for the controller for the bed, just managing to grasp it between the tips of his fingers. Once he was sitting up he felt a little better, and a cup of tea from the breakfast trolley consolidated the improvement. If he lowered the height of the bed a little, he could reach the locker door, and he found a couple of T-shirts, a hooded top and some sweatpants stacked neatly inside.

'Hey…' One of the nurses, whom he knew by sight, was marching across the ward towards him. 'What are you doing?'

'Mobilising.' He gave her a smile and she ignored it.

'Ah. Not playing with the controls on the bed, then.' She picked up the remote, and hooked it on the end of the bed, out of reach.

'Nah. I wouldn't dare.' He tried the smile again, and this time the nurse grinned back. 'But I would like to get out of bed. Have a wash and get dressed.'

'I don't know. You're not supposed to…'

But he was going to. Jon knew exactly what he wanted to say to Chloe, and he couldn't say it like this. He needed to get back on his feet, and the sooner he started, the sooner he'd get there.

'Please.' He flashed the nurse his most winning smile. 'I promise I won't overdo things.'

'All right. Stay there, I'll go and get a wheelchair.'

Jon couldn't help watching the doors of the ward and as the hands of the clock closed on the number twelve he operated the controls of his bed to put him as close to a sitting position as possible. It was crazy. Chloe wouldn't be here this early. She might not be here at all, in which case he'd go and find her, as soon as he was able. But when the first group of visitors came onto the ward she was one of them, a large bag slung over her shoulder and Amy in her arms.

'You're dressed. And sitting up.' She grinned in approval.

Amy was looking at him intently, and Jon wondered

whether his swollen and bruised eye was frightening her. He covered it with his hand and smiled at her, his eye throbbing with pain.

'Hurt… Kiss it better.' She looked enquiringly up at Chloe.

'Yes, sweetie. You want to kiss it better?'

Amy nodded, and Jon held out his hands towards her. Chloe delivered her into his arms, and he hugged her tight.

'Careful, now, sweetie.' Chloe caught Amy's reaching hand just before it connected with his face. 'We have to be very gentle with him.'

Amy seemed to understand. Stretching up in his arms, she planted a kiss on his cheek, and Jon struggled to keep his composure.

'Thank you, Amy. That feels much better now.' He stroked the little girl's light auburn curls and she snuggled into his arms.

'Would you like to give Jon his get-well parcel?' Chloe sat down on the moulded plastic chair next to his bed and opened her bag.

The parcel was wrapped in sparkly blue and gold paper, which was obviously designed to appeal to Amy. The little girl sat on the bed next to him and Chloe placed the parcel into her lap. She slid one finger under the wrappings, and slowly started to tear them.

Chloe grinned. 'No, Amy, it's for Jon. Give it to him.'

Amy pretended not to hear and Jon leaned over. 'You're going to unwrap it for me, aren't you?'

He helped her with the sticky tape, holding her tight so she didn't slip off the bed, and hoping that none of the nurses saw them and came to tell him that a child really shouldn't be sitting on his bed. Chloe seemed to have the same thought and turned, pulling the curtains a little so that they weren't immediately visible from the door.

Inside the parcel was a book and a packet of chocolate buttons. Amy left the book for him and picked up the chocolate.

'Hey, that's lovely, Amy. Thank you.' He picked up the book and Amy handed him the chocolate buttons, clearly wanting him to open them and give them straight back. He shot Chloe an enquiring glance, wondering if it was all right for Amy to have the chocolate.

'Just a few.' She pressed her lips together in wry humour. 'The chocolate's from me. Amy chose the book.'

He laughed, ignoring the painful protest from his eye. 'She likes whodunnits, does she? Thank you, Chloe.'

Thank you for the book and the chocolate, and for wrapping them up. For bringing Amy. For yesterday, and for being here today. Thank you for being so beautiful.

'You're welcome.'

He was sure now. Chloe and he weren't perfect for each other, they were different in so many ways. But while perfect was nice, wanting was everything. And Jon knew beyond any shadow of a doubt that everything he wanted was here now. He would get out of here, get himself back together and win her back.

She came again on Sunday, this time alone. Amy and Hannah had gone to James's for lunch, and it was clear that Chloe had missed the family gathering to come and see him.

'So they're letting you out today?'

'Looks like it. I'm waiting for the duty doctor to sign me off, and then me and my crutches are free to go.'

He indicated the pair of crutches that were propped up behind his chair.

'So—how long?'

Jon grinned. 'Who knows? I offered to sign myself off, but the nurses didn't think much of that suggestion.'

'No. Don't suppose they did. Well, I'll wait and take you home.'

'I can get a taxi.' He didn't want to push things just yet.

'Don't you dare.' She got to her feet. 'I'm going to go and ask where the doctor is. Has the pharmacy sent up your drugs yet?'

'Not yet.'

'Then I'll see what I can do to chase them up, too.'

Chloe's enquiries seemed to bear more fruit than his, possibly because she was able to follow people and buttonhole them, rather than having to wait for them to come to her. It took another hour, but by two o'clock he was being wheeled to the hospital entrance by a porter, his possessions packed into a plastic bag. He waited on a bench beside the automatic doors, which delivered a blast of cold air every time someone walked through them, and when he saw Chloe's car draw up outside he got carefully to his feet.

She got him into the car and was on the main road, driving away from the hospital, before she dropped the bombshell. 'You're coming home with me for a decent meal. And you can stay the night. Hannah and Amy are staying over at James's tonight, so you can take their room.'

In her house. Surrounded by her scent. That wasn't a good idea. He needed to be stronger before he could even think about putting his plan into operation.

'Thanks, but... I'm okay. I'd really like to go home.'

'So you can lie in bed and look at the hole in the ceiling? Hannah told me that your bedroom's a right mess.'

'I've got a sofa-bed downstairs, I'll sleep there.' He grinned at her. 'Save me going up and down the stairs for a few days.'

'You can't camp out in your own house, Jon. It's much more comfortable at my place...'

The discussion rumbled on for the duration of the drive to her house. But Chloe had the last word because she was the one driving, and Jon couldn't do anything about where she chose to take him. It was an unfair advantage but Chloe would take whatever she could get.

She helped him out of the car and he carefully negotiated the front path and the step over the threshold and into the house. It seemed that he'd at least reconciled himself to a meal, if not a bed for the night, but she could work on that.

Leading him into the sitting room, she fetched a footstool and a cushion so he could prop his leg up.

'Would you like some tea? Or coffee?' She was trembling suddenly. Being alone with him was different from the bustle of the hospital, where caring was the normal course of action and not a choice.

'Let me—'

'No, you've only just sat down. Don't be silly.' Chloe was feeling more and more nervous. This wouldn't do.

His eyes softened, as if he saw her anguish, and she felt herself redden. This was no time to be thinking about the emotional, she had to think about the practical.

'Chloe, I've got to be able to do things for myself. Let me try, please.'

She felt her legs begin to shake. Before she could

stop it, a tear ran down her cheek. 'No. No, you can't, Jon. I won't let you.'

'Why not?'

'Because…' *Just because.* That was the best answer she could think of, but the worst one was the one that spilled out before she could stop it 'Because I know you're trying to be independent and look after yourself, and that's a good thing. But I know how much that hurts, too. I know you were afraid when you were alone up there in the loft with a broken leg because I was afraid when I was alone here, all the times I fell over and couldn't get up.'

'Yeah. I was afraid.'

'So why won't you let me look after you a bit? Just stay here for a few days, until you're a bit stronger.'

A shadow passed across his face. She'd blown it all, but suddenly Chloe didn't care. Doing nothing wasn't an option, not any more.

'It's too soon…'

It was always going to be too soon for Jon. There was never going to be a right time. But she could bear that now. She could bear him walking away from her, but what she couldn't live with was never having tried.

'I don't care. It doesn't matter if you're never going to want me the way I want you, and I don't expect anything from you. I just want to be there for you.'

'Chloe…' He struggled to his feet. He was going to go now, she knew it. Even though she'd steeled herself to it, the idea seemed to suck all of the air from the room, and she couldn't breathe.

All the same, she went to help him. If he wouldn't stay here, it would be just as well if he didn't break the other leg.

'Chloe.' She'd given him his crutch and he'd got his

balance now, but he still didn't let go of her shoulder. 'I meant that I'm not well enough to try to win you back. Not yet. But I will…'

He pulled her against him, holding her tight. She could hear his heart beating. Or was it hers?

'What do you mean, you're not well enough? You think I want you to run up and down the stairs ten times?'

'Just the once would be good…' Suddenly everything had changed, and Chloe gave him a playful dig in the ribs. Jon winced, smiling.

'Sorry… Bruises?'

'It doesn't matter. This isn't how I wanted it to be, I wanted to give you flowers and be able to get down on my knees and beg…'

'You know you don't have to do that. I love you. More than I'm afraid of losing you.'

'I love you too. More than I'm afraid of messing this up.'

He kissed her, puffing out an exasperated breath when he wobbled a little and she had to steady him. Then he smiled down at her and Chloe reached up, gently pulling him down for another kiss. This was exactly how it was meant to be. Not caring about who was supporting who, but just stronger together.

'I wish I could sweep you off your feet. There are so many things…' He kissed her brow, his mind obviously working overtime to catalogue the many things.

'Don't keep it to yourself. Tell me about it.'

'The thing I most want right now?' He smiled down at her. 'I just want to hold you, Chloe, and feel your skin against mine. But I'm not sure I can stand up for very much longer.'

Helping him up the stairs and into her bedroom

wasn't exactly what either of them might have fanta-
sised about, but it was perfect. Settling him on the bed,
propping his leg on a pillow and stripping off his sweat-
shirt felt like the most romantic thing in the world, as
did having to stand a little to one side to let him see
her pull her top off, because his left eye was pretty
much closed.

'You'll take me like this?' His fingers brushed the
bruises on his left side. 'They're not very pretty.'

'It's just a few bruises. They make you look ruggedly
pretty.' Chloe climbed onto the bed, careful not to touch
him, but he chuckled, pulling her close.

As she settled against him he let out a contented sigh.
All the missing and the longing had been set free, with
only love left to replace it.

When he finally spoke, she could hear the smile in
his voice. 'So how long do you reckon we'll be able to
hold out for?'

He'd been thinking the same thing she was. Her body
was buzzing with warm arousal, but the urgency was
slaked by the knowledge that Jon was in no condition
for anything other than rest right now. And they had a
future. They didn't need to rush things.

'I can hold out for a very long time, Jon.'

'Really?'

'Yes, really. You're recovering from a nasty injury,
and you need to rest.' She said the words with as much
determination as she could muster. 'We're going to have
to take things slowly and gently. A little improvisation
maybe…'

He chuckled. 'I'm looking forward to seeing what
improvisations you'll come up with.'

She looked up into his face, feeling the love that

she saw there reverberate in her heart. 'Are you going to behave or am I going to have to be strict with you?'

Jon pulled her down for a kiss. 'You're going to have to be *very* strict, my love.'

CHAPTER NINETEEN

One year later...

THE LAST YEAR had been...interesting. Jon had needed another minor operation on his leg, and it had taken a while before he'd been fully fit again. Hannah had studied hard and completed the whole of her correspondence course in time to sit her Art A-Level in June, and had then panicked on the day of the exam. Chloe had marched her into the examination room and sat outside to make sure she didn't escape, and when Hannah received her results, she'd passed with flying colours.

Amy was a bright, secure toddler, who brought joy to both her mother and to her aunt and uncle. They'd all moved into the new house together, and Amy loved the bright room with the animal mural.

And Jon and Chloe had been married in the spring. It had rained all day, but the warmth and love had shone through. Despite everything, they were blissfully happy.

Once every month they'd take turns in booking a surprise destination for a date night. The destination wasn't a surprise this time, though. By the time they'd reached Dover Chloe knew exactly where Jon was taking her. It had been a year, to the day, since the night they'd spent at the chateau in France.

It was just the same as before. They dressed up and sat on the roof for dinner. When the table was cleared and they went back downstairs, a bottle of champagne was waiting for them in an ice bucket.

'One year.' Chloe wound her arms around his neck, standing on her toes to kiss him. 'It's been the happiest of my life.'

'Mine too. But next year's going to be better.'

'I think so too.'

He leaned towards her, whispering in her ear. 'I'll always love you, Chloe. Whatever happens, my life with you is perfect.'

There was just one thing missing. They'd been trying for a baby since their wedding night and Chloe knew how much Jon wanted to be a father. She desperately wanted a child of her own too.

'I have something for you.'

'I don't know what you could possibly give me, sweetheart. I have everything I'll ever want.'

'No, you don't. But we will have…' She took his hand between hers, and placed it over her stomach.

'Chloe? You mean…?'

'A baby. We're going to have a baby.'

He stared at her for a moment, as if he didn't quite comprehend. And then he hugged her tight, his limbs trembling. When he kissed her, she saw tears in his eyes.

'We did it, Jon. It took a little while, but we made a baby.'

He lifted her off her feet, holding her tight against his chest. 'We're going to have such fun. We'll get her a train set. Or him…'

Jon had been thinking about this. So had she, and finally it had happened. 'You've been planning ahead.'

'I might need some time to try it out first. Just to make sure it works.'

'Good idea. I love you so much.'

'I love you too. And over the next week I'm going to show you just how much…'

'The next week?'

'Didn't I mention that? Since you probably knew that we were coming here, I decided that I owed you another surprise. So I spoke to your head of department, and he agreed to give you a week's leave. You can sign the leave slip when you get back.'

'A week! Are we staying here?'

'Wait and see. Anything could happen. But right now…'

She was ready for it all. And the best thing about that was that Jon was here, and he was ready for it too.

'Right now everything's perfect.'

He shook his head, smiling. 'No. Not perfect. It's so much better than perfect.'

* * * * *

*If you enjoyed this story, check out these
other great reads from Annie Claydon*

*ENGLISH ROSE FOR THE SICILIAN DOC
THE DOCTOR'S DIAMOND PROPOSAL
RESCUED BY DR RAFE
SAVED BY THE SINGLE DAD*

All available now!

MILLS & BOON®

MEDICAL ROMANCE™

THE ULTIMATE IN ROMANTIC MEDICAL DRAMA

A sneak peek at next month's titles...

In stores from 27th July 2017:

- **Tempted by the Bridesmaid** *and*
  Claiming His Pregnant Princess – Annie O'Neil

- **A Miracle for the Baby Doctor** – Meredith Webber
  and **Stolen Kisses with Her Boss** – Susan Carlisle

- **Encounter with a Commanding Officer** –
  Charlotte Hawkes
  and **Rebel Doc on Her Doorstep** – Lucy Ryder

Just can't wait?
Buy our books online before they hit the shops!
www.millsandboon.co.uk

Also available as eBooks.